The Unraveling

Jaxon Dorne

Introduction

The rain had been falling since dawn, a slow, steady drizzle that turned the roads to dark ribbons of wet asphalt. Dana Crowell sat in her childhood home, staring at the stack of old notebooks spread across the kitchen table. Letitia Clark's scribbled notes, her mother's fading journal entries—remnants of the past year that had shaped her in ways she could hardly put into words.

Tomorrow was the funeral.

Evelyn Crowell had fought for as long as she could. The sickness had come slowly at first, a persistent fatigue that Dana had dismissed as grief. But the whispers had returned, pressing in at the edges of their home, and with them, her mother's health had deteriorated rapidly. In the end, it wasn't just illness that took her—it was something deeper, something older, something that had been waiting.

The doctors called it pneumonia. Dana knew better.

One year had passed since the night she had faced the Mother of Pines. Since she had fought to reclaim her home, to push back against the cycle of disappearances that had plagued Pine Hollow for decades. Amanda Hastings had been found, delirious and covered in pine needles, whispering the name of a girl who had been missing for fourteen years. Morgan Reece, Dana's childhood best friend—the girl whose disappearance had marked the beginning of everything.

The ritual had worked. For a time.

She had thought they were free of it. That she had pushed the presence back, sealed it away with iron and salt and whispered names. But as the months dragged on, the weight of what she had done never fully lifted. The forest never truly let go.

Her mother had felt it first. The slow return of something unseen, the growing pressure in the air. She had begun speaking less, watching the windows more, waking in the night to whisper warnings Dana couldn't bear to hear. The fever had come after that, draining her strength, leaving her frail and frightened. In the end, she had died in her sleep, her final breath a whispered plea.

"Don't let them in."

Now, with the funeral looming, Dana felt the weight of it pressing against her chest. The town had moved on, willing itself to forget, but Dana knew the truth. It wasn't over.

Sheriff Ben Reese had been the only one who had believed her last year. The only one who had seen what she had seen. They had kept in touch, but as the months passed, he had grown quieter, more cautious. He wanted to believe the danger had passed.

Dana wasn't so sure.

A gust of wind rattled the window, and she turned her head sharply, heart pounding. The trees swayed in the distance, dark silhouettes against the gray sky.

She closed her eyes, breathing deeply. She would get through the funeral. She would bury her mother and face the whispers and the empty condolences.

Chapter 1

Dana Crowell stood over her mother's grave, the chill seeping into her bones as the wind whispered through the pines. The sky sagged under the weight of gray clouds, heavy and unrelenting. Pine Hollow's cemetery was old—too old—its crooked headstones and weather-worn statues softened by time. A cluster of mourners lingered a few yards away, silent, their eyes fixed on her. But their expressions weren't just grief-stricken. There was something else beneath the mourning—a quiet, uneasy suspicion.

As if Evelyn Crowell's death wasn't just an end, but a warning.

"Don't let them in."

"Don't let *them* in."

Dana kept thinking back to her mother's final words.

Dana wasn't sure what to make of the plurality in her mother's plea. Was she referring to the whispers as more than just a piece of the Mother of Pines, or was the Mother of Pines something else entirely?

The priest's voice droned in the background, his prayers lost to the wind. The casket descended, swallowed by the earth, and Dana's fingers twitched at her sides. An absurd, impossible urge gripped her—to stop it, to pull the coffin back up, to refuse this finality. But it was too late.

It had been too late long before today.

A light touch at her elbow made her jolt. Sheriff Ben Reese stood beside her, his presence steady, solid. She hadn't even heard him step closer.

"You okay?" he asked, voice low. They both knew the answer.

Dana parted her lips to answer, but something flickered at the edge of her vision. A figure. Tall. Still. Wrapped in a dark coat just beyond the tree line.

She turned sharply.

Nothing. Just swaying branches, the woods shifting with the wind. A trick of the light? Exhaustion?

Then why did the back of her neck prickle like she was still being watched?

One by one, the mourners drifted away, their footsteps fading over brittle grass and damp earth.

Dana stayed.

The mound of fresh dirt loomed before her, stark against the older graves. Final. Unforgiving. The weight of her mother's absence pressed deep into her bones. The wind still whispered through the pines—a sound that had always unsettled her.

Ben lingered too. Watching. Waiting. Like he wasn't sure if she wanted company or an escape.

"I can drive you back," Ben murmured.

Dana shook her head. "Just a minute."

Her voice was steady. Her insides weren't. A minute wouldn't bring her mother back. A minute wouldn't fix anything. But she couldn't leave yet—not while Evelyn was still above the earth, still waiting to be buried by time.

Ben exhaled softly, his boots crunching over the dirt as he stepped back. Giving her space, but not distance. He never strayed too far.

The cold pressed deeper into her skin. Dana barely felt it.

Her eyes stayed fixed on the fresh dirt, on the ground swallowing her mother whole. This was loss. The slow, inevitable unraveling she had seen coming for years.

And yet, standing here, she felt something else. Something older than grief.

A hollow place. A place where time stretched thin, where the dead weren't entirely gone.

A gust of wind curled through the trees, carrying the damp scent of earth—and something else. Something metallic.

Dana stiffened. Just the forest. Just her mind playing tricks. She had spent her childhood surrounded by these trees, hearing the stories, feeling their weight press in on Pine Hollow like an unspoken warning. She had once believed leaving town was the only way to escape their pull.

Now, standing here again, she wasn't so sure.

Her breath came slow and measured as she stepped back from the grave. The instant her boot left the disturbed earth, the hush deepened. The air pressed in around her, waiting, listening.

She turned toward the gate. And then—just as she crossed the boundary of the burial ground—

A whisper.

Faint. Almost nothing. Or maybe... a voice.

Her mother's voice.

Dana froze mid-step, her pulse hammering.

Hold still. Listen.

The cemetery remained deathly silent. Only the wind moved, threading between the headstones. *It's nothing. Just grief twisting the ordinary into something sinister.*

Then why did it still feel like someone was here?

Slowly, she turned her head, scanning the graves. Nothing. The fresh mound of dirt looked the same, stark against the older, timeworn markers. Her mother was beneath that soil. That was all.

So why couldn't she shake the feeling that something was watching?

Crunch.

Not the wind. Not an animal. A footstep.

Dana spun.

A man stood at the edge of the cemetery, just past the wrought-iron gate.

Not a mourner.

His coat was thick, collar turned up against the cold. A hat obscured most of his face. But even from here, she could feel his stare. Unblinking. Heavy.

He didn't move. Didn't speak.

Just watched.

"Dana?"

Ben's voice cut through the quiet.

She flinched, snapping toward him. Too fast. Too sharp.

When she turned back—the man was gone.

Her stomach clenched. Impossible. The gate was too far. He couldn't have disappeared that quickly. Could he?

"I'm fine," she said. The lie sat thin on her tongue.

Ben didn't buy it. His eyes flicked to the empty space where she'd been looking. "You sure?"

She hesitated. Then forced herself to nod. "Yeah." Another lie.

"Let's go."

She didn't look back.

Didn't let herself.

But as she climbed into her car and pulled onto the road, the unease coiled tight in her chest. Whoever—whatever—had been standing there... she could still feel them watching.

The drive home was suffocatingly silent.

The trees pressed in on either side of the road, their skeletal branches tangling together like reaching hands. Dana gripped the wheel tighter, forcing herself to focus. Not on the man. Not on the cemetery.

But the question twisted inside her anyway.

Had he really been there? Or was she seeing ghosts now, summoning shadows where none existed?

Stress. Grief. Exhaustion. That had to be it.

Ben's cruiser followed, his headlights cutting through the mist.

She considered pulling over. Telling him.

But what would she even say? *I saw a man who wasn't there?*

He was already watching her too closely, waiting for her to unravel.

And maybe she was.

By the time she reached the driveway, shadows had swallowed the Crowell house.

It looked the same. Weathered clapboard. Sagging porch. Pine needles clinging to the roof like the house had grown them itself.

But it felt different.

Like it had been holding its breath.

The wind stirred as Dana climbed out of the car. The porch swing groaned, swaying back and forth.

Slow. Rhythmic.

The wind wasn't strong enough to move it.

Ben pulled in behind her, shutting off his engine but making no move to leave his car just yet. Instead, he watched her, waiting. Dana exhaled, rolling her shoulders before heading toward the house. She had barely set foot on the first porch step when a familiar scent hit her—smoke.

Faint, like old wood burning, curling through the crisp air. Her brow furrowed as she turned toward the forest, her eyes narrowing into the dark.

She knew that smell. It was the same scent she had woken up to the night Morgan disappeared.

The realization sent a slow, crawling chill down her spine.

Ben finally climbed out of his car, shutting the door softly behind him. "What is it?"

Dana hesitated, shaking her head. "Nothing." Another lie. She was already collecting them like stones in her pocket. She didn't know what she expected to find if she stared at the woods long enough, but a part of her—a part she didn't want to acknowledge—felt like something was staring back.

She turned her back on the trees and stepped up onto the porch. The floorboards groaned beneath her weight, the sound oddly familiar. How many times had she run up these very steps as a child, feet light with the careless energy of youth? Now, they felt heavier, like the house was reluctant to let her inside.

She reached for the doorknob, but stopped.

The door was already unlocked.

Dana stared at the door, her pulse quickening. She was certain she had locked it before leaving for the funeral. The house had been empty—no visitors, no reason for anyone to be inside. And yet, the door hung just slightly ajar, a sliver of darkness visible beyond the threshold. She swallowed hard, resisting the instinct to step back. This was her mother's house. Her house now. If someone was inside, she wasn't about to let them cower in the shadows while she stood frozen on the porch.

Ben must have noticed her hesitation. His boots clunked against the wooden steps as he came up behind her. "Dana?" His voice was low, cautious. He saw it too.

Without answering, she pushed the door open. The hinges let out a tired groan, the sound reverberating through the dim interior. The air inside was thick with dust and something else—something faintly metallic, like rust or blood. Dana hesitated only a moment before stepping in, flicking on the light. A weak glow illuminated the foyer, casting long shadows that stretched toward the hallway. Nothing looked disturbed. The furniture was as she had left it, the air still and quiet. But that did nothing to shake the uneasy feeling curling in her gut.

Ben stepped in behind her, one hand resting lightly on his hip, where his holster sat. His gaze swept the space, practiced, methodical. "Anything missing?" he asked.

Dana's eyes darted over the living room—the threadbare couch, the framed photos coated in dust, the antique clock on the wall, its hands frozen at a time that had long since passed. "No," she said slowly. "But something's off."

She moved toward the kitchen, running her fingers along the edge of the table as she went. Everything was in its place—the dish rack, the old kettle, the stack of unopened mail her mother had never gotten around to sorting. But then she saw it. A single chair, pulled out just slightly from the table. Dana stopped, her breath catching in her throat.

"I didn't leave it like that," she murmured.

Ben followed her gaze, his expression hardening. He didn't need to ask if she was sure. Instead, he stepped forward, brushing a finger against the tabletop. "There's dust everywhere, except here," he muttered, indicating a faintly clean spot where a hand might have rested. "Someone's been here recently."

A flicker of unease passed through Dana. "But why?" she asked, more to herself than to Ben. If someone had broken in, why wouldn't they have taken anything? Nothing was rifled through, nothing disturbed—except that chair. It was almost like someone had been sitting there, waiting.

A sudden noise from down the hall made her jump—a soft creak, like weight shifting on old floorboards. Both she and Ben went rigid. Her eyes snapped to the hallway leading toward her mother's bedroom.

Ben's hand went to his gun.

Dana's pulse pounded as she took a slow step forward.

"Dana," Ben warned.

She ignored him, forcing herself to move. The hallway stretched long and dark, each step dragging her deeper into the house. The door to her mother's room was slightly ajar, just like the front door had been. Her fingers curled into a fist as she reached out and nudged it open.

The room was empty.

But the closet door stood wide open.

And inside, scratched into the wooden frame, was a single word:

LEAVE.

Dana's breath caught as she observed the word engraved into the closet's wooden frame. The letters were jagged, uneven, like they had been scratched in a hurry—or with something dull, something not meant for carving. The gouges looked fresh, the raw wood pale against the darkness of the closet's interior. A rush of cold air prickled over her skin, though she wasn't sure if it was real or just the creeping dread settling into her bones.

Ben stepped past her, his body tense, his gaze scanning the room. "This wasn't here before?" he asked, already knowing the answer.

"No," Dana whispered. The truth of it settled heavy in her stomach. Someone—or something—had been inside this house, inside her mother's room. They had left a message, deliberate and unmissable. But why? Was it a warning? Or something worse—an invitation?

Ben reached into the closet, running his fingers over the fresh carvings. His jaw tightened. "These aren't old," he muttered. "Wood's still splintered at the edges. This was done recently." He turned to Dana. "You're sure the house was locked before you left?"

"Yes," she said quickly, but the moment the word left her lips, she faltered. Had it been? She had been in a haze of exhaustion, grief, and unease when she left for the funeral. Had she double-checked the locks? She wanted to believe she had, but doubt curled in her gut like smoke.

Ben exhaled, stepping back from the closet. "Whoever did this wanted you to see it. And if they got in once, they can get in again." He turned toward her, his expression firm. "You're not staying here alone tonight."

Dana opened her mouth to argue, but no words came. The weight of the house, of the moment, pressed down on her. Every instinct screamed at her to get out, to step away from whatever unseen presence was twisting its way through the walls. But leaving meant running, and she wasn't ready to do that—not again.

She swallowed hard and forced herself to look away from the message, instead focusing on the room itself. It felt emptier than it should, as if something vital had been drained from it. The air smelled stale, untouched, yet she could feel the presence of someone who had stood here, someone who had taken the time to carve those letters into the wood.

"Do you think it was just some sick prank?" she asked, though she knew how flimsy the question sounded.

Ben's expression darkened. "No," he said simply. "This isn't kids messing around, Dana. This is someone sending a message."

A silence stretched between them, thick with tension. The air in the house felt colder than before, like the walls themselves had absorbed the weight of what had been written. She didn't want to admit it, but she wasn't sure she wanted to sleep here tonight—not with that word carved into the wood, not with the image of the man at the cemetery still burned into her mind.

Finally, she sighed. "Fine," she muttered, rubbing a hand over her face. "I'll get a bag. But just for the night."

Ben nodded, satisfied, and stepped back to give her space. "I'll wait outside," he said. "Keep an eye out."

Dana nodded absently, already moving toward her old bedroom. As she passed through the hallway, she felt the hairs on the back of her neck rise. She paused, glancing over her shoulder. The closet door was still open, the carved word glaring back at her like an open wound.

LEAVE.

She shivered and turned away, forcing herself to keep moving. As she entered her childhood bedroom, she hesitated, suddenly uneasy. Everything was exactly how she had left it years ago—the same faded wallpaper, the same creaky wooden dresser, the same bed that now seemed too small for her. But something about the room felt... off.

The air was thick with dust, but the floorboards near the window looked disturbed, faint scuff marks where no one should have been. And then she saw it—something sitting on the center of the bed. A single pine needle, resting atop the sheets like a deliberate offering.

Dana's stomach twisted. She didn't touch it. She didn't move.

Somewhere outside, the wind howled through the trees, carrying with it the sound of something that almost—almost—sounded like laughter.

Dana didn't touch the pine needle. She didn't need to. Its presence alone was enough to unnerve her. She had spent too many nights as a child waking to find the scent of pine clinging to her clothes after dreams she couldn't quite remember. This was deliberate. Someone—something—wanted her to see it.

She forced herself to turn away, grabbing her old duffel bag from the closet and shoving in a change of clothes, her toothbrush, and a few other essentials. Her hands moved on autopilot, but her mind kept circling back to the needle, the scuff marks on the floor, the open closet in her mother's room. None of this made sense. Was someone trying to scare her out of town? If so, they were doing a damn good job.

A floorboard creaked outside her door. Dana's breath caught, and she spun toward the sound, heart hammering. Ben stood just outside the threshold, his face shadowed in the dim hallway light. He held up a hand, placating. "Didn't mean to sneak up on you," he said. "But you were taking a while."

Dana exhaled, her pulse still uneven. She zipped up her bag and slung it over her shoulder. "I'm good to go," she muttered, brushing past him.

Ben followed her down the hall, his presence steady behind her. He didn't say anything as she locked the front door behind them, but she could feel his gaze flicking toward the house, scanning the dark windows as if expecting something—or someone—to be watching from within.

As Dana stepped onto the porch, a gust of wind cut through the trees, carrying with it the faintest echo of something she almost recognized. A voice. A whisper. She shivered and quickened her pace toward her car.

Ben opened the passenger side door of his cruiser and nodded toward the seat. "Come on," he said. "You can stay at my place tonight."

She hesitated, gripping her bag's strap tighter. "I can get a motel."

He scoffed. "Yeah? The closest one is forty minutes out, and I doubt you'll get any sleep there. Not after today."

Dana wanted to argue, to push back against the concern in his voice, but she was too damn tired. The adrenaline from the past few hours had begun to fade, leaving her with a bone-deep exhaustion she couldn't shake. The thought of being alone in a cold motel room, with nothing but her thoughts and the sound of the wind creeping through the trees, didn't seem any better than the alternative.

She exhaled, giving in. "Fine." She climbed into the cruiser. "But just for the night."

Ben shut the door behind her before rounding the car and sliding into the driver's seat. He didn't say anything as he pulled onto the road, but Dana caught the way his knuckles tightened on the steering wheel. He was on edge, too.

Neither of them spoke as the car rolled past the looming treeline. But as Dana stared out the window, watching the forest blur by, she could have sworn she saw a shape standing among the trees—tall, motionless, watching.

She blinked, and it was gone.

The ride to Ben's house was quiet, the low hum of the cruiser's engine the only sound between them. Dana stared out the window, her fingers absently tracing patterns against the fabric of her duffel bag. The weight of the day sat heavy on her shoulders, but her mind refused to settle. Her mother's funeral, the unlocked door, the word carved into the closet, the pine needle—all of it churned together, an unease she couldn't shake.

Ben didn't push her to talk, but she could feel his eyes flick toward her every so often. He wasn't just watching her—he was watching the road, the trees, everything around them like he was expecting something to emerge from the darkness. It should have made her feel safer, knowing he was on alert, but instead, it only reinforced the gnawing feeling that something was wrong.

Finally, he broke the silence. "You really think someone broke in just to scratch a word into the closet?"

Dana sighed, rubbing her temples. "I don't know what to think." She hesitated before adding, "Nothing else was touched. No valuables gone, no sign of forced entry. It's like they didn't come to take anything." She let out a slow breath. "Just to leave a message."

Ben's grip on the steering wheel tightened. "That's what bothers me."

Dana glanced at him. "You don't think it was just some asshole trying to scare me off?"

His jaw flexed. "Maybe. But that means someone in town knew you were coming back before today."

The thought hadn't occurred to her. She had only returned this morning, straight to the funeral, barely spoken to anyone outside the cemetery. How would someone have known to get inside her mother's house, let alone leave a message that specific?

Goosebumps prickled along her arms. Someone had been waiting for her.

Ben's house sat on the outskirts of Pine Hollow, a modest one-story with a deep porch and a garage that looked like it hadn't been used for anything but storage in years. The yard was mostly gravel, the treeline looming at its edges. Dana had only been here once, years ago, before she left town. It looked almost the same, except for the addition of a new security light flickering against the porch.

He pulled into the driveway and cut the engine. For a moment, neither of them moved.

"You staying in the car all night, or are you coming in?" Ben asked, trying for a smirk, but there was tension behind it.

Dana rolled her eyes, pushing open the door. "I'm thinking about it."

The air was colder here, or maybe that was just in her head. As she grabbed her bag from the backseat, she found herself glancing toward the trees at the edge of the property. There was no movement, no obvious sign of anything lurking. But the longer she looked, the more unsettled she felt. Like something was there, just waiting for her to stop looking.

She forced herself to turn away. Not tonight. Not now.

Inside, the house was warm, smelling of old wood and faint traces of coffee. Ben flicked on a lamp, casting a soft glow over the living room—a simple space, neat but lived-in. A leather couch, a scuffed-up coffee table, a shelf lined with books and old case files. She caught sight of a framed photo near the kitchen doorway, a younger version of Ben in his police academy uniform, standing beside a man she assumed was his father.

"You can take the couch or the guest room," Ben said, tossing his keys onto the counter. "Up to you."

Dana hesitated. The guest room was fine, but something about sleeping behind a closed door, alone, left her uneasy. "Couch is good," she muttered, dropping her bag beside it.

Ben didn't argue. He just nodded, heading toward the kitchen. "You want coffee? Something stronger?"

She let out a dry laugh. "You got something stronger?"

He smirked. "I might."

Dana sank onto the couch as he rummaged through a cabinet. The tension in her shoulders eased just a little, but her mind wouldn't stop churning. She knew she should be exhausted, but something inside her remained on edge, like her body knew sleep wasn't an option tonight.

Her gaze flickered toward the window. The porch light cast a faint glow over the yard, the gravel driveway, the first line of trees beyond it. And for just a moment—just long enough to make her doubt herself—she thought she saw a shadow move between the trunks.

When she blinked, it was gone.

Ben returned a moment later, setting two glasses on the coffee table. Dana didn't ask what was in them—she just reached for one and took a sip, welcoming the slow burn of whiskey as it slid down her throat. It helped, even if just a little. She let her head rest against the back of the couch, staring up at the ceiling as Ben dropped into the chair across from her.

"You planning on telling me what's really going through your head?" he asked, his voice casual but edged with concern.

Dana sighed, swirling the liquid in her glass. "Honestly? I don't know." She leaned forward, resting her elbows on her knees. "Something about all of this just doesn't sit right. My mother's death, the break-in—if that's even what it was—and that damn message in the closet. It's like… I don't know. Like something's circling me, just waiting."

Ben watched her carefully. "You think someone in town is trying to push you out?"

Dana hesitated before shaking her head. "No, it's not just that. I mean, yeah, I wouldn't put it past some of them to want me gone, but this feels different." She paused, searching for the right words. "It's like whatever this is, it's been waiting. I haven't been back in years, but the second I step foot in Pine Hollow, things start happening."

Ben didn't answer right away. He took a slow sip from his glass, gaze drifting toward the window. His expression was unreadable, but Dana could tell he was considering something—something he wasn't sure he wanted to say out loud.

"What?" she asked, watching him closely.

For a moment, he didn't move. Then, finally, he set his glass down with a quiet clink. "I've been sheriff for almost ten years now," he said, voice low. "And in that time, I've learned that things in this town don't just happen."

Dana's skin prickled. "What do you mean?"

Ben leaned forward, resting his arms on his knees. "Strange things, Dana. Things that don't make sense. Reports of people seeing things that shouldn't be there—shadows in the woods, figures standing in places they disappear from too fast. Kids saying they hear voices calling their names when no one's around. And then there are the disappearances." His jaw tensed. "People vanish in this town. Always have. Some we find explanations for, but others…" He shook his head. "Others we don't."

A heavy silence settled between them. Dana gripped her glass tighter. This wasn't just about her mother's house, or the message in the closet. Ben had been sitting on something much bigger—something he clearly hadn't wanted to acknowledge until now.

"You're saying this has been going on since I left?" she asked, her voice quieter than she meant for it to be.

Ben exhaled through his nose. "It's been going on for a hell of a lot longer than that."

Dana sat back, her heart pounding against her ribs. She had grown up hearing the whispers, the town's hushed stories about the woods, the unspoken rules about where not to go after dark. But she had always chalked it up to superstition, small-town paranoia.

Now, staring at Ben, seeing the exhaustion lining his features, she wasn't so sure.

"Why are you telling me this now?" she asked.

Ben met her gaze, something unreadable flickering in his eyes. "Because I think whatever this thing is—whatever's been waiting—it's not done yet."

Outside, beyond the glow of the porch light, something moved in the trees. It was slow, deliberate, almost like it was listening.

And then, just as quickly, it was gone.

Dana's grip tightened around her glass, her knuckles turning white. "So what, you think this thing—whatever it is—came back because I did?"

Ben shook his head. "I don't think it ever left." He rubbed a hand over his jaw, sighing. "But you showing up might've stirred it up again. It's been quiet for a while—at least, as quiet as Pine Hollow ever gets. Then your mother dies, you come back, and suddenly, someone—or something—is inside her house leaving messages in closets." He leaned back in his chair. "That doesn't feel like coincidence to me."

Dana swallowed, the whiskey doing nothing to warm the cold creeping up her spine. "You ever get close to figuring out what it is?" she asked, voice lower now.

Ben didn't answer right away. Instead, he stood, crossed the room, and grabbed a thick file from a shelf near his desk. He dropped it onto the coffee table in front of her with a heavy thud. The cover was worn, the edges creased, but Dana could see a name scribbled in marker across the top. Morgan Reece.

Her throat went dry.

She hesitated before reaching for it, running her fingers over the name of the friend she had lost nearly two decades ago. She glanced up at Ben, waiting for an explanation.

"I pulled this out of archives when your mom passed," he said. "Figured you'd ask eventually." He sat back down, watching her carefully. "But there's something in there I don't think you ever knew about."

Dana slowly flipped the file open, her breath catching as she saw Morgan's missing person's report—the grainy school photo, the basic details. It was a document she had seen before, back when she was younger and desperate for answers. But Ben was right. Something was different this time.

A sheet of paper was clipped to the back, yellowed with age. It wasn't a police report. It was a journal entry.

She scanned the words, her pulse climbing. The handwriting was messy, rushed, but she could still make it out.

April 6, 2010—Morgan Reece, age 14, last seen near the woods behind the Crowell house. Witness (Dana Crowell) states she heard Morgan calling her name from the forest before she disappeared. Searched area thoroughly. No sign of struggle, no tracks leading away. No footprints leading in.

Dana felt the blood drain from her face.

She barely remembered giving that statement. She had been hysterical, barely coherent, desperate for someone to believe her. And when no one found Morgan, they all assumed the same thing—she had run away, left town, slipped into the night like a ghost. But reading it now, something else stood out.

"No footprints leading in," she whispered.

Ben nodded grimly. "Like she was already in the woods before she ever walked in."

A heavy silence stretched between them. Dana's heartbeat thudded against her ribs as she stared at the paper, her mind spinning. Had Morgan ever left the woods that day? Or had something taken her before she even had the chance?

She exhaled shakily, closing the file. "What are you saying, Ben?"

Ben's expression was unreadable, his voice steady but dark.

"I'm saying maybe Morgan never left."

The wind outside picked up, rustling through the trees. The porch light flickered, dimming just slightly. The house creaked, old wood settling—or something else shifting just beneath the surface.

Dana didn't move. She barely breathed.

Somewhere, deep in the woods, something whispered her name.

Dana swallowed hard, her fingers still curled over the edges of the file as if letting go of it would somehow make the words inside disappear. But they wouldn't. They were burned into her brain, the implications sinking in like ice beneath her skin. She had spent years convincing herself she had misremembered that night, that grief and panic had distorted what she thought she saw—what she thought she heard.

But now? Now she wasn't so sure.

She glanced up at Ben, at the way the lamplight cast shadows along his jaw, at the way his eyes—steady, unwavering—watched her. He was waiting for her to process it, to react. But she wasn't sure how. The air between them felt charged, something more than the weight of their conversation hanging in the space. It was in the way he leaned forward, the way his knee brushed against hers beneath the coffee table, the way neither of them moved to break the contact.

"I don't know what to do with this," she admitted, her voice quieter now, rougher.

Ben's eyes flickered, his gaze dipping for the briefest second—to her mouth, then back up. The moment was so quick she almost doubted it had happened, but the shift in the air told her otherwise. He wasn't just concerned about her. He never had been.

He exhaled, rubbing a hand over the back of his neck. "You don't have to do anything tonight," he said, his voice lower than before. "You should get some sleep. We'll figure out what this means in the morning."

Dana let out a hollow laugh, sinking back into the couch. "Sleep? Yeah, sure. Like that's gonna happen."

Ben smirked, just a little, and for a brief moment, it felt like they were somewhere else—somewhere before all of this, before ghosts and missing friends and pine needles left as warnings. He was still looking at her like he was debating something, something he wasn't sure he should say, but Dana could feel it between them, the unspoken weight pressing in.

He leaned back slightly, but he didn't move away from her completely. "You're sure you don't want the guest room?"

Dana scoffed, but the corner of her mouth lifted just slightly. "And leave you out here all alone, paranoid about whatever's in those woods?" She tilted her head, her voice teasing now. "You sure you don't want me to take the couch?"

Ben huffed a quiet laugh, but his eyes darkened just a fraction, something unreadable flickering in them. "I think I can handle one night."

Dana arched a brow. "You sure?"

For a beat, neither of them moved. The tension between them stretched thin, electric, humming beneath the surface of everything else. The kind of pull that had always been there, buried beneath years of silence and unresolved history, now rising between them in the dim light of his living room.

She wasn't sure which of them was going to break it first.

The sound of the wind outside cut through the moment, a sharp gust against the windows. Dana forced herself to breathe, to pull back before she did something stupid—before they did something stupid. She had too much shit to sort through, too much rattling around in her head.

She grabbed her glass and downed the last of her drink, letting the burn center her. "I should probably get some rest," she muttered, though she wasn't sure she believed herself.

Ben nodded, but the muscle in his jaw ticked. "Yeah. Probably."

But neither of them moved.

Ben exhaled, running a hand through his hair as he stood. "I'll grab you a blanket," he muttered, heading toward the hallway.

Dana nodded, still gripping the empty glass in her hand. She felt off-kilter, not just from the weight of what she'd read, or the creeping unease that had settled in her bones since she'd arrived in town, but from something else. Something unspoken that had thickened the air between them in a way she hadn't expected.

When he returned, he tossed a folded blanket onto the couch beside her. "If you need anything, the guest room's down the hall," he said, voice neutral, unreadable. He lingered for half a second longer than necessary before finally turning away.

"Yeah," she murmured. "Got it."

She watched him disappear down the hall, the quiet click of his bedroom door closing behind him.

Dana sat there for a long time, staring at the darkened TV screen, the whiskey settling warm in her stomach. The silence of the house pressed in on her, heavy, thick, as if something unseen lurked in the corners, waiting for her to close her eyes. She knew it was irrational—Ben's house was safe, solid, locked up tight. But she felt it anyway. That familiar presence, the one she had always sensed just beyond her reach.

She rubbed at her temples, trying to will away the buzzing in her head, but it wasn't just the alcohol making her restless. It was everything. Her mother's death. The break-in. The whisper of her name in the woods. The fact that Morgan's disappearance had never really left her, no matter how much time had passed.

And underneath it all—deep in her gut—was that same old pull. A force she couldn't name, couldn't explain, something more than grief, more than exhaustion. It clawed at her, nudging her toward something she wasn't sure she wanted to acknowledge.

Before she could talk herself out of it, she stood.

Her bare feet were silent against the hardwood as she crossed the house. The hallway stretched ahead of her, dimly lit from the bathroom's nightlight, her pulse beating a little too fast.

She wasn't thinking clearly. Or maybe she was. Maybe she was thinking more clearly than she had in years.

The door to his room was closed, but she hesitated only a moment before pushing it open.

Ben was lying on his back, his arm resting against his forehead, the blankets half kicked off. The soft glow from the window cast shadows over his face, his chest rising and falling in slow, even breaths.

He stirred, blinking blearily at her, but he didn't sit up. Didn't tell her to leave. He just watched her, his expression unreadable.

Dana swallowed. She should have left. She should have said never mind and turned around, gone back to the couch, forced herself to sleep. But the words never came.

Instead, she stepped forward, letting the door click shut behind her.

She wasn't sure who moved first. Maybe it was him. Maybe it was her. But in the next breath, there was no space between them.

It wasn't soft. It wasn't delicate. It was desperate—grief-soaked and electric, a collision of old tension and something neither of them had been willing to name before now.

His hands were warm against her skin, her breath hitching as his fingers curled at the base of her spine, pulling her closer. She didn't stop him. She didn't want to stop him.

And for a little while, the weight of Pine Hollow, of everything that had been haunting her, disappeared into the dark.

The Next Morning

Dana woke before dawn, the room still cloaked in shadows. The weight of the blankets was unfamiliar, as was the warmth of the body beside her.

She blinked, the events of the night crashing down on her all at once.

Ben was still asleep, his breath even, his features soft in the early light. She could feel the heat of him, the reality of what they had done settling into her bones. But before she could let herself think too hard about it, she slipped out of bed, pulling the sheet around her as she moved toward the door.

By the time Ben woke up, she was already in the kitchen, dressed, pouring coffee into one of his chipped mugs. She didn't look at him when he entered, and he didn't say anything about it.

But the tension was still there, thick and heavy, lingering beneath the surface like something neither of them were ready to touch just yet.

"Coffee's ready," she muttered.

He nodded, rubbing a hand over his face before reaching for a mug. "Thanks."

And just like that, they let it sit. Ignored. But not forgotten.

Not even close.

Chapter 2

Ben pulled a thick binder from the shelf near his desk, its cover worn from years of handling. He dropped it onto the coffee table between them with a dull thud, flipping the cover open without preamble. Inside were dozens of laminated case files, reports yellowed with age, some bearing faded handwriting in the margins. Dana frowned, running her fingers over the edges of the pages.

"You've been holding onto this for a while," she muttered, glancing up at him.

Ben nodded, leaning forward with his elbows on his knees. "Started collecting them when I first joined the department. Back then, I thought it was just old-town superstition, people seeing things that weren't there. But the more I looked, the more I saw patterns." He flipped to a marked page, his brow furrowed. "Same locations. Same descriptions. Decades apart."

Dana scanned the file he had opened, her eyes catching the familiar headline: LOCAL TEEN MISSING AFTER VENTURING INTO WOODS. The date stamped at the top read March 15, 1982. The photo below it showed a young girl, no older than sixteen, her smile frozen in time.

"The details line up," Ben said, tapping the file. "Last seen near the forest's edge. No signs of a struggle, no tracks leading in or out. Just gone." He flipped to the next page, another case, nearly identical. September 9, 1954. Another teenager, same circumstances, same location. Then another. And another.

Dana's stomach twisted. "This isn't random."

Ben shook his head. "No. And it's not just kids." He flipped toward the back of the binder and pointed to a newer file. "This one was from before I became sheriff—2006. A guy named Mark Atwood. He was twenty-six. Local. Went hunting with friends. They found his rifle. His pack. But not him."

Dana exhaled slowly, flipping through the files. Some were thin, no more than a single page. Others were thick with attached witness statements, grainy photographs, reports from officers long since retired. She skimmed one labeled December 1971—a woman in her forties had vanished from her own backyard, only fifty yards from her house.

She frowned. "What's the longest gap between disappearances?"

Ben rubbed his jaw. "Fifteen, maybe twenty years at most. And then, every time, it starts up again."

Dana felt a chill creep up her spine. She turned another page, her hands slowing as she reached one of the oldest reports in the binder. It was different from the others. Handwritten. No official letterhead, just aging paper and slanted script.

November 1892.

She read the first few lines and felt her stomach drop.

The trees took him.

Dana's fingers hovered over the fragile paper, careful not to smudge the ink. The handwriting was spidery and uneven, the kind that belonged to someone writing in a hurry—or in fear. She read the words again, heart pounding.

The trees took him.

She glanced up at Ben. "This isn't a police file. Where did you get this?"

Ben shifted in his chair. "An old sheriff's journal. Found it buried in the archives when I was digging into the town's missing persons records. Back then, things weren't as official as they are now. Some of these cases didn't make it into any official reports." He nodded toward the page. "Keep reading."

Dana turned her attention back to the entry, the ink faded but still legible.

November 3, 1892

We searched the woods for three days. No trail. No blood. The dogs refused to track beyond the clearing. They whined, tails tucked, would not enter. I have seen many things in my years, but never this. The trees took him. The woods swallowed him whole. And I fear we will never find him.

Her mouth went dry. "Who was 'him'?"

Ben flipped to the next page, revealing another document—this one typed, but still old, the paper brittle with age.

"Joseph Harlan," Ben said, tapping the name at the top of the page. "A logger who worked the forest perimeter. One night, he went out to check his traps. Never came back." He pulled out another sheet, placing it next to the first. "A month later, his wife swore she saw him standing in the woods. She described it exactly the same way every witness since then has—just standing there, still, watching. When she called his name, he turned and walked back into the trees."

Dana exhaled sharply. "And they never found him?"

Ben shook his head. "Not a trace."

She leaned back, raking a hand through her hair. "So we have a pattern of people disappearing for over a century, no bodies ever found, and multiple witnesses claiming to have seen the missing afterward?" She gestured toward the pages in front of them. "This isn't a serial killer. This is something else."

Ben hesitated before nodding. "That's what I've been thinking too."

The words settled between them like a weight. Dana didn't want to admit it out loud, but the implications were clear. This wasn't just a series of vanishings—it was a cycle. Something embedded in the bones of Pine Hollow, repeating over and over again.

She flipped back to the 1982 case. "Who was the last person to disappear?"

Ben's expression darkened. He reached toward the binder and pulled out a thinner folder, one Dana hadn't seen yet. When he placed it in front of her, she felt the breath leave her lungs.

Morgan Reece.

Her best friend. The one who had disappeared right in front of her.

She forced herself to open the file, but her fingers trembled as she lifted the top page. She had been interviewed as a teenager, barely able to process what had happened at the time. The official report was sparse, clinical.

April 6, 2010. Witness states she heard Morgan Reece calling her name before the victim disappeared. No sign of forced abduction. No footprints found leading away. Investigation remains open.

Ben watched her closely. "You were the only one who heard her that night."

Dana nodded slowly, gripping the paper tighter. "Yeah." She hesitated before adding, "But I don't think I was the only one who saw her."

Ben frowned. "What do you mean?"

She swallowed. "My mother."

Ben sat forward. "You think she saw something?"

Dana nodded, a memory surfacing from the depths of her mind—one she had buried for years. The night Morgan vanished, after the frantic search, after the police combed the woods and found nothing, Dana had returned home. Her mother had been waiting. Pale. Silent. Her eyes hollow, like she had seen a ghost.

Dana had asked if she thought Morgan had run away. Her mother had hesitated—just for a second—before saying, Some people don't run. Some people just… disappear.

At the time, Dana had thought it was just grief, just her mother's way of trying to make sense of something that made none. But now, sitting here, looking at these files, the unease settled deep in her stomach.

Her mother had known something.

And now, she was gone too.

Dana took a deep breath, closing Morgan's file. "We need to get back to the house."

Ben didn't argue. He just stood, grabbed his keys, and nodded. "Let's go."

Ben grabbed his jacket from the back of the chair, slipping it on as Dana gathered the files into a neat stack. She didn't know why she felt the need to be careful with them—maybe because they were more than just records. They were pieces of people, remnants of lives that had been cut short by something no one seemed to understand. And now, she and Ben were following their ghosts.

She tucked the binder under her arm as she followed Ben to the door. Outside, the morning sun had risen higher, but it did little to cut through the biting cold. The trees stood tall in the distance, unmoving, the wind failing to rustle their branches. It was the kind of eerie stillness she had learned to ignore as a child but now found impossible to dismiss.

Ben stopped at the driver's side of his cruiser, resting his hand on the roof. "Before we go," he said, looking at her with something close to reluctance, "I need to ask—are you sure you want to do this?"

Dana frowned. "What kind of question is that?"

"You know what kind," he muttered, rubbing a hand over his jaw. "You left this place for a reason. I'm giving you one last chance to turn back before we start digging into things we might not be able to walk away from."

She studied him for a long moment. He wasn't just worried about her—he was worried about what they might find. About what they might wake up.

But Dana already knew there was no turning back.

She had come home, and something had been waiting.

She tightened her grip on the files and walked toward the cruiser. "I'm not leaving," she said simply, climbing into the passenger seat.

Ben sighed but didn't argue. He got behind the wheel, started the engine, and pulled onto the road.

Neither of them spoke as the town faded behind them, the trees stretching taller, darker, as they neared her mother's house.

The ride was silent, but tension lingered thick between them. Dana stared out the window, watching the landscape roll by. Some things had changed in Pine Hollow—new businesses, freshly paved roads—but the woods had stayed the same. They had always been there, always watching, always waiting.

As they turned onto the dirt road leading to the Crowell house, Dana felt a familiar pressure settle in her chest. She hadn't been back in years, but the house looked almost exactly as she remembered. The peeling paint, the sagging porch steps, the way the windows reflected nothing but empty sky.

Ben slowed the car, his grip firm on the steering wheel. "No sign of forced entry from the outside," he noted. "Still doesn't mean much."

Dana nodded, staring at the house. In the daylight, it should have felt less intimidating. Less wrong. But instead, she felt something worse.

The house wasn't just waiting for her.

It was expecting her.

Ben parked, but neither of them moved to get out right away. Dana took a slow breath, steadying herself.

"Alright," Ben muttered. "Let's see what's inside."

Dana opened the door, stepping out onto the gravel driveway. The wind had picked up slightly, carrying the scent of damp earth and pine. She hesitated for only a moment before making her way toward the front steps.

As she reached for the doorknob, she noticed something she hadn't last night.

The door was locked.

Her stomach turned. She knew, knew she had left it unlocked after they found the message in the closet. But now, it was shut tight, the deadbolt engaged.

Ben noticed too. He pulled his gun from its holster, his expression unreadable. "Someone's been here."

Dana's pulse pounded in her ears as she reached into her pocket and pulled out her key.

She slid it into the lock, turned it, and pushed the door open.

Inside, the house was silent.

But it wasn't empty.

The air inside the house was thick—stagnant, heavy, as if it hadn't been disturbed in years. But Dana knew that wasn't true. She had stood in this very spot just last night. And now, something had changed.

Ben stepped in behind her, his grip firm on his gun. His eyes scanned the entryway, the living room, and the narrow hallway that led toward the kitchen. Dana forced herself to focus, to ignore the way the silence pressed in around them.

"Anything look different to you?" Ben murmured, low enough that his voice barely disturbed the quiet.

Dana took a slow step forward, her eyes darting over the details of the house. The furniture was exactly where it had been before. The photos on the wall, the books on the shelves—untouched. But something still felt off.

Then she saw it.

The chair at the kitchen table—pushed back, just an inch further than before.

Dana swallowed hard. "That chair—"

Ben followed her gaze, his expression tightening. "It moved."

It shouldn't have been enough to make her stomach twist, but it did. Someone—or something—had been here. Had sat at that table. Had left no other trace of their presence except for this small, deliberate shift.

Ben moved first, stepping into the kitchen, gun lowered but ready. Dana followed, her skin crawling as she approached the table. She placed her fingers on the chair's back, pushing it lightly. It rocked against the floor, softly, deliberately, like a response.

She gasped.

The refrigerator door was slightly open.

She frowned. "Did you—?"

Ben shook his head. He stepped forward, reaching for the handle and pulling it open the rest of the way.

Dana's stomach dropped.

Sitting on the top shelf, where butter or leftover groceries should have been, was a single pine cone.

Ben grabbed it, turning it over in his hands. It was small, perfectly intact, the kind that littered the forest floor by the thousands. But not inside a fridge. Not here. Not like this.

Dana exhaled slowly. "That wasn't there before."

Ben nodded grimly. "No, it wasn't."

Neither of them moved for a long moment.

Finally, Ben shut the fridge, his expression unreadable. "Let's keep looking."

They moved cautiously, sweeping through the rooms one by one. The living room—untouched. The bathroom—same as before. Her mother's bedroom—the closet still open, the word LEAVE carved into the wood glaring at her like an accusation.

Finally, they reached her old bedroom.

Dana hesitated before stepping inside. The air felt different here—thicker, colder as if the walls themselves had absorbed something over the years. The bed was still made, the furniture arranged the same way she had left it before she moved away.

But then she saw the dresser.

Something had been placed on top of it.

A pine cone.

Just like the one in the refrigerator.

Her breath left her in a slow, controlled exhale. She felt Ben step in behind her, but she couldn't take her eyes off it.

"It wasn't there before," she murmured.

Ben moved closer, his expression dark. He reached out, touching the edge of the dresser near the pine cone. A thin smear of dust clung to his fingers, except for the spot where the object sat—as if it had been placed there recently.

"Someone's leaving these for you," he muttered.

Dana's pulse pounded in her ears. "Why?"

Ben didn't have an answer. Neither did she.

But whoever had been inside the house hadn't taken anything. They hadn't damaged anything. They had only... left something behind.

A sound creaked from down the hall.

Both of them froze.

It had come from the basement.

Dana's chest tightened. Slowly, she turned toward the hallway, her feet moving on instinct. The door was closed, just as it had been when they entered. But the air had changed.

Something was waiting for them down there.

Ben tightened his grip on his gun. His voice was barely above a whisper.

"Tell me you locked that door last night."

Dana's hands clenched into fists.

"I don't think I ever opened it."

Dana stared at the basement door, heart pounding. It looked the same as it had the night before—plain wood, slightly warped with age, the old brass handle dulled from years of use. But something about it felt different now. The air around it was heavier, charged with something unseen.

Ben stood beside her, his posture tense, his grip tightening around his gun. He hadn't drawn it yet, but the way his fingers flexed told her he was considering it. That more than anything unsettled her. Ben wasn't the type to rattle easily.

"You ready?" he murmured.

Dana nodded, but her throat was dry. She reached for the doorknob, forcing herself to grip it even as her instincts screamed at her to stop. The metal was cold—too cold.

She twisted the knob and pushed the door open.

The scent hit her first.

The basement had always smelled musty, like damp wood and old stone, but now there was something else. A faint metallic tang—rust or blood. The air was thick with it, stale and unmoving.

Ben flicked on the light. The bulb at the bottom of the stairs sputtered weakly, hesitating before casting a dim, yellowish glow. Shadows pooled in the corners, stretching unnaturally against the walls. The wooden steps groaned beneath Dana's weight as she descended, each one creaking like a warning.

She reached the bottom first, her boots touching the cold concrete floor. The space looked the same—shelves lined with old boxes, an unused workbench in the corner, the old furnace still looming against the far wall. But even before Ben joined her, Dana knew.

Something had been down here.

Her eyes moved across the room, searching for anything out of place. Then she saw it.

One of the boxes had been pulled off the shelf, its contents scattered across the floor. Papers, old photographs, scraps of faded newspaper. A few were crumpled, smeared with dust—like someone had been searching for something.

Ben stepped forward, sweeping his flashlight over the mess. His movements were slow, deliberate. Dana followed, her unease sharpening as she took in the scene. Nothing else seemed disturbed—just this. Just this box.

Then—the lightbulb popped.

A sharp, sudden crack split through the silence.

Shards of glass rained down, some bouncing off the floor near Dana's boots. The basement was instantly plunged into darkness.

Dana sucked in a breath, heart leaping into her throat.

Ben cursed under his breath, already reaching for the flashlight on his belt. A second later, a beam of stark white cut through the pitch-black, illuminating the workbench, the shelves, and the furnace hunched like a shadowed figure in the far corner.

"Well, that's great," Dana muttered, forcing her pulse to slow. "Perfect timing."

Ben swept the light across the basement. "Probably just an old bulb."

Dana exhaled through her nose. "Yeah. Probably."

But even as she said it, she didn't believe it.

The sudden plunge into darkness had unnerved her more than she wanted to admit. It was too abrupt, too perfectly timed with their descent.

Ben crouched near the mess, shifting through the loose pages. His fingers brushed over an envelope tucked beneath a few yellowed newspaper clippings. He pulled it free, turning it over in his hands.

The handwriting on the front was unmistakable.

Evelyn Crowell.

Dana's breath caught. She reached for it, fingers trembling slightly as she traced her mother's familiar script. It wasn't just a random letter—it was addressed to her.

Her name was scrawled across the front.

She hesitated.

Why would her mother have hidden a letter down here? And why had someone been searching for it before they got here?

Ben's voice was low. "You gonna open it?"

Dana stared down at the envelope, her mother's handwriting frozen in time. Her name was scrawled across the front in hurried strokes, as if Evelyn had been rushed—or afraid.

Her fingers trembled slightly as she tore it open. The paper inside was brittle, yellowed at the edges, but the ink was still dark, bold, urgent.

She swallowed hard and began to read.

Dana,

If you're reading this, it means you've come back. I hoped you never would. I hoped you'd stay far away from this place. But if you're here, then you need to listen to me.

They never stopped watching you.

I tried to keep you safe. I tried to keep them away. But they always come back, Dana. And now that you're here, they know. They've always known.

You have to go. Get out of Pine Hollow. Get as far as you can before it's too late.

If you don't...

They'll take you too.

Dana's breath came shallow, her grip tightening around the paper. The words blurred as she reread them, her mother's warning sinking into her bones.

She felt Ben step closer. "What does it say?"

She handed him the letter, her pulse thundering as he scanned the page. His jaw tensed, and when he finished reading, he let out a slow, measured breath.

"Your mom thought something was after you," he muttered.

Dana clenched her fists. "Not just after me. Watching me."

Ben ran a hand down his face, processing. "Alright," he said finally. "This could mean a lot of things. Maybe she was paranoid, maybe she—"

"No." Dana's voice was firm, her skin crawling with certainty. "This isn't random. This isn't grief, or paranoia, or some dying woman's delusion." She gestured at the scattered papers around them. "She was documenting something. Keeping records."

She swallowed. "And someone was looking for them."

Ben's flashlight beam traced over the mess. A faint streak cut through the layer of dust on the floor, a disturbance in the dust trail—like something had been dragged. His eyes narrowed.

Dana followed his gaze. The streak led toward the corner.

Right to the furnace.

A slow, icy dread settled in her stomach.

Ben moved forward first, the beam of his flashlight steady. Dana followed, her breath shallow. The old furnace was large, its rusted metal covered in dust. She had always hated it as a kid—its hulking, hollow shape, the way it would rattle late at night, like something was shifting inside.

Ben crouched, sweeping the light lower. His expression darkened.

"Dana," he murmured. "Look."

She stepped closer—and her heart stopped.

At the very bottom of the furnace door, peeking out just slightly, was the edge of a piece of cloth.

A sleeve.

Dana's pulse roared in her ears.

Ben reached out, grabbing the furnace handle. It groaned as he pulled, the old metal screeching. The door yawned open.

Inside, tucked into the shadows, was a jacket.

A child's jacket.

Small, faded from time, its blue fabric barely visible beneath the dust and grime.

Dana knew that jacket.
She remembered it.
It was Morgan's.

Chapter 3

The silence stretched between them, thick and suffocating. Dana's fingers were still curled around the dust-covered jacket, her breath shallow as she tried to process what she was seeing. Morgan's jacket. Here. Hidden in the furnace for sixteen years.

Ben stood beside her, his flashlight beam steady on the old fabric. His expression was unreadable, but his jaw was tight, his grip firm around the handle of his gun. He was waiting—for her reaction, for her to say something, for an explanation that neither of them had.

Finally, Dana exhaled and shoved the jacket into a plastic evidence bag Ben handed her. "Someone put this here," she muttered. "And I don't think it was my mother."

Ben's brow furrowed. "Then who?"

Dana swallowed. "That's what we need to find out."

Back upstairs, the air in the house felt different. Heavier. Like the discovery had unsettled something beyond just Dana and Ben. She locked the evidence bag in the back of Ben's cruiser while he made a call to have the jacket analyzed for DNA, though she doubted they'd find anything useful.

Dana leaned against the car, arms crossed. "We're missing something."

Ben pocketed his phone. "Someone in town knows more than they've said." He glanced at her. "Who would your mom have trusted enough to talk about this?"

Dana thought for a moment. Her mother had been quiet and withdrawn in her later years. But if there was one person who might have had answers—or at least suspicions—it was Miriam Delacroix.

"She ran the town's historical society," Dana said. "But she was more than that. She and my mother were close for a while."

Ben nodded. "You think she knows something?"

Dana let out a slow breath. "I think she knew my mother was afraid of something. And I think it's time we find out what."

Miriam Delacroix's Home – A House of Secrets

Miriam Delacroix lived on the outskirts of town in a house that had been old when Pine Hollow was young. It sat at the end of a long dirt driveway, half-swallowed by trees, its wraparound porch sagging under the weight of time.

As Ben pulled into the driveway, Dana felt a familiar unease crawl along her skin. She had been here before, years ago, when her mother used to drag her along for afternoon tea and whispered conversations. Even then, she had sensed something strange about the house.

Miriam herself was a relic. A woman in her seventies, but sharp-eyed and quick-tongued, someone who had seen too much and spoken of too little.

Dana stepped onto the porch and knocked.

For a long moment, nothing.

Then, the sound of slow, deliberate footsteps.

The door creaked open just enough for Miriam Delacroix to peer out at them. Her silver hair hung loose, wisps curling wildly around her face as if she hadn't bothered to tame it in days. But it wasn't her appearance that made Dana's stomach tighten.

It was what she was holding.

A small bundle of twigs, wrapped in red twine, the ends blackened as if they had been burned. She clutched it tightly in one hand, the other resting lightly on the doorframe, her nails yellowed but clean. The smell of smoke and something faintly herbal drifted from inside the house.

Miriam's sharp blue eyes flicked between them, lingering on Dana for a long moment before shifting to Ben.

"You should have stayed away," Miriam said softly.

She didn't make a move to open the door further. If anything, she seemed reluctant to let them in at all.

Dana's throat went dry. "You know why we're here."

Miriam didn't answer right away. Instead, she let out a slow breath and, with deliberate care, reached up to the doorframe, where a small sprig of dried herbs hung above the entrance—sage, rosemary, and something Dana didn't recognize.

Then, still holding the charred bundle in her hand, Miriam stepped aside.

"You'd better come in," she murmured. "Before they know you're here."

Dana stepped over the threshold, the weight of Miriam's words settling into her chest. *Before they know you're here.*

The house smelled exactly the same as she remembered. Old wood, dried herbs, and something earthy, almost like rain-soaked stone. But beneath it all was a familiar note—chamomile and orange peel.

Her childhood tea.

Dana's throat tightened. It could have been a coincidence, but she doubted it.

Miriam had been expecting her.

Ben followed behind his presence, grounding. Miriam closed the door and slid the deadbolt into place. Not just the handle lock—the deadbolt.

Dana caught the flicker of movement as Miriam's hand brushed over a small metal charm tacked above the doorframe. She didn't acknowledge it, but Dana saw it for what it was.

A ward.

Miriam moved toward the sitting room, her long skirt whispering against the floor. The house was cluttered but precise—shelves stacked with books, some so old their spines had faded completely. The fireplace sat unlit, but the ashes in the hearth were fresh like something had burned there recently.

Dana noticed small bundles of herbs tied with twine hanging from nails near the windows. Some she recognized—sage, rosemary. Others, she didn't.

Miriam settled into a worn armchair, watching Dana with an unreadable expression.

"I take it this isn't a social call," she murmured.

Dana let out a breath. "No. We found something."

Miriam's sharp gaze flickered between her and Ben. "Of course you did."

She didn't sound surprised.

Dana pulled the evidence bag from her coat pocket and set it on the coffee table. Morgan's dust-covered, time-worn jacket sat folded inside.

Miriam's expression didn't change, but Dana didn't miss the way her fingers curled slightly against the armrest. A slight, almost imperceptible stiffening of her spine.

For a long moment, she said nothing.

Then, finally, she leaned forward, reaching out—not to touch the bag, but to trace a shape in the air just above it—a shape Dana couldn't quite make out.

When Miriam looked up, there was something darker in her eyes.

"Where did you find this?"

Dana hesitated. "The basement. In the furnace."

Miriam closed her eyes, exhaling through her nose.

Then, so softly Dana barely heard it, she whispered—

"She tried to hide her."

Dana's grip on her emotions was slipping.

Miriam's whispered words—She tried to hide her—sent something hot and sharp surging through Dana's chest.

She had spent years burying this pain, years forcing herself to forget. But now, standing in this house, staring at a woman who knew more than she was saying, the weight of it all threatened to crack her wide open.

Dana shot forward, slamming her hands down on the armrests of Miriam's chair.

"No more riddles, no more cryptic bullshit!" she snapped, voice raw. "Tell me the truth, Miriam! All of it. What did my mother know? What did you know?"

Ben shifted beside her, his body tensing, but he didn't intervene. This wasn't his fight.

This was between Dana and Miriam.

Anyone else would have been met with Miriam's sharp tongue, a biting retort that cut straight to the bone. She had never been one to tolerate outbursts, let alone demands. If it were anyone else—Ben, a town council member, even Evelyn in her final years—Miriam would have lashed back with ferocity, shutting them down with a look, a few well-placed words that left no room for argument.

But this was Dana.

And Miriam could see it—the fire in her, yes, but also the cracks forming beneath it. The fear. The kind that opened doors that should stay closed.

And fear was how they got in.

So Miriam did something rare. She softened.

She reached out, her weathered hands warm, and cupped Dana's face—just for a moment. Not forceful, not demanding. Steady.

Her voice, when she spoke, was low, calming.

"Breathe, child," she murmured. "Don't let them see you like this."

Dana froze.

Miriam's hands weren't as rough as she expected. They were warm, grounding. A sharp contrast to the rising panic clawing up Dana's throat.

Don't let them see you like this.

It wasn't just a phrase.

It was a warning.

Dana's stomach twisted. She clenched her jaw, forcing herself to breathe, to shove down the flood of emotions threatening to consume her.

She was not a child anymore. She would not be weak.

Miriam watched her carefully, waiting for Dana's pulse to slow and for her to take back control.

Then, when she saw the moment Dana steadied herself, her expression changed.

The mystery, the evasiveness—it all fell away.

Miriam sighed, finally leaning back in her chair.

"I'll tell you what I know," she murmured. "But you have to understand, Dana…"

She looked toward the window, at the trees beyond.

"Some truths will break you."

Miriam let out a slow, measured breath as if weighing whether Dana was ready to hear what she had to say. Her fingers curled slightly against the armrest, her sharp gaze scanning Dana's face, searching for cracks, weaknesses—anything that might make her hesitate.

"You have to understand," she said, her voice quieter now and steadier. "Some things, once known, can't be forgotten. And once you see them for what they are—they never stop looking back."

Dana's pulse thumped in her ears. "I don't care."

Miriam studied her a moment longer, then nodded, as if she had expected that answer. She glanced toward the window, where the treetops swayed in the windless afternoon. Then, finally, she spoke.

She hesitated, then spoke again. "The Mother of Pines… she's not a woman. Not a single being. That's just how the stories made sense to people. The truth is worse. She's them. All of them. The Watchers. The ones who take, who erase. The ones who are always watching."

Dana's stomach dropped. "Then she's not real?"

"Oh, she's real," Miriam murmured. "Just not in the way you thought. She's every voice that's been lost, every memory wiped clean. She's the name they gave the ones who decide who stays and who disappears."

"Your mother wasn't trying to protect you from her, Dana." She leaned forward, voice dropping lower. "She was trying to protect you from them."

The room felt smaller.

Dana's breath stilled in her throat.

There it was again—that same word, the one that had been following her like a shadow since she arrived.

Them.

The letters carved into her mother's closet. The whisper in the woods. The way the town had felt wrong the second she returned.

Miriam's gaze flickered to Ben, just for a moment, before settling back on Dana. "How much do you remember about the night Morgan disappeared?"

Dana opened her mouth automatically, ready to recite the same story she'd told the police a thousand times.

But then—

A flicker.

The scent of pine needles and damp earth.

Morgan laughing, just ahead of her, disappearing behind a tree. "Dana, wait—"

The snap of a branch, but too far away. Not where Morgan had gone.

Then silence.

And the feeling that someone else was there.

Watching.

Dana blinked hard, her vision snapping back to Miriam's study. Her breath came uneven, her pulse too fast.

Miriam was still watching her, waiting.

"They don't just take people, Dana," she said softly. "They take pieces of them. The pieces that let you remember."

Dana's fingers curled into fists. The missing memories. The gaps in the story she had never questioned until now.

"Who are they?" she forced out.

Miriam exhaled, rubbing a hand over her knees, and for the first time, she looked old.

"You've seen them," she murmured. "Even if you don't realize it yet."

Another flicker—

The trees were bending the wrong way, though there was no wind.

A figure in the distance. Not Morgan. Not human.

The feeling that if she turned too fast, she'd see something she wasn't supposed to.

Dana gritted her teeth, shoving the memories down. "Just tell me."

Miriam leaned in, eyes dark. "Your mother tried to stop them. She tried to hide Morgan from them. But she failed."

Dana swallowed. "And now?"

Miriam sighed, shaking her head. "Now that you're back, Dana…"

She looked straight at her, her eyes heavy with meaning.

"They know."

Dana clenched her jaw, trying to ignore the prickling sensation at the back of her neck—the way the room felt heavier, denser, as if the very air had thickened. It wasn't just Miriam's words getting to her. Something else was pressing in.

Her mind rebelled against the flickering images that had surfaced. The gaps in her memory. The way the woods had swallowed Morgan whole.

And now, Miriam was telling her that her mother had known. Had tried to stop it. Had failed.

Dana forced herself to speak, even as her throat felt tight. "What did my mother do?"

Miriam hesitated, pressing her lips together like she was debating how much to say. Then, finally, she sighed.

"She tried to keep you out of it," she said. "Tried to make sure you wouldn't remember enough to go looking." Her gaze flickered to the letter still sitting on the table. "But something changed. She must have known her time was running out."

Ben, who had been silent all this time, finally stepped forward. "How long has this been happening?" His voice was steady, but Dana could tell he was struggling to reconcile what he was hearing.

Miriam glanced at him, then back at Dana.

"You've seen the files," she murmured. "You know this didn't start with Morgan."

Dana's stomach twisted. "How far back?"

Miriam's fingers tapped against the armrest of her chair, a slow, rhythmic movement. A hesitation.

She exhaled through her nose. "Long before this town had a name."

Silence.

A deep, settling silence, like the very walls were holding their breath.

Dana tried to process that. The disappearances, the patterns—they went back centuries.

She rubbed a hand over her face, exhaling sharply. "Why Morgan?" Her voice cracked slightly. "Why not me?"

Miriam's gaze softened, and for the first time, Dana saw something like regret in her expression. "I don't know," she admitted. "But I do know this—"

She sat forward, eyes locked on Dana's.

"If you keep digging, if you keep remembering, they will come back for you."

The words settled in Dana's bones like ice.

Then—

A sound.

Faint. Distant.

From outside, beyond the house.

A whisper.

Dana's name.

Dana didn't move.

The whisper had been soft, almost fragile, carried on air that shouldn't have reached inside the house. It shouldn't have reached her.

But she didn't react. Didn't even let her breath hitch.

She could feel the weight of Miriam's gaze, steady and sharp, studying her, waiting to see if she'd break. If she'd acknowledge it.

Dana clenched her fists beneath the table. Don't let them see you like this.

She forced her voice to stay level. "So what am I supposed to do?"

Miriam leaned back in her chair, fingers drumming against the wood. "You could leave."

Dana let out a bitter laugh. "We both know that won't change anything."

Miriam's expression didn't shift, but she didn't argue.

Ben, still standing near the fireplace, crossed his arms. "Then what? We do nothing?"

Miriam glanced at him, and Dana swore she saw something like pity in her eyes. "You think action is the answer."

Ben narrowed his gaze. "It usually is."

Miriam shook her head. "Not with them."

Dana swallowed, the whisper still crawling in the back of her mind. "Then what?"

Miriam hesitated. Then she sighed, standing slowly, her joints creaking like the house itself. She moved toward the shelf in the corner, running a hand over the spines of ancient books, fingers hovering over one bound in dark, weathered leather.

Finally, she pulled it free.

She turned back to Dana, holding it out.

"If you want to survive this, you need to understand what you're dealing with."

Dana stared at the book. The cover was unmarked, no title, no name. The edges were rough, the binding worn like it had passed through too many hands.

She reached for it.

And for just a second—the air around them felt too still.

Miriam didn't let go immediately. Her fingers lingered on the book as Dana took it, her grip light but deliberate.

"Read carefully," Miriam murmured. "And don't let them know you're reading at all."

Dana's pulse ticked up, but she nodded, tucking the book into her jacket.

Miriam sighed, looking tired in a way that went beyond age. "That's all I can give you."

Dana wanted to argue. To demand more. But Miriam had already told her more than most ever would.

And she could tell—there were things she wouldn't say, no matter how much Dana pushed.

The wind outside shifted suddenly.

Miriam's head snapped toward the window. Just for a second.

Then, she turned back. "You should go."

Dana didn't argue.

Ben didn't either.

Without another word, they stepped outside, into the waiting dusk.

The moment Dana stepped over the threshold, out into the dimming light, something shifted.

The air outside was thicker, heavier, pressing against her skin in a way it hadn't before. It wasn't just the change from inside to out—it was the feeling of leaving something behind.

Miriam's house had felt small, enclosed, secretive—but safe. Not in a way that meant they were untouchable, but in a way that meant whatever was outside had to wait.

Now, it wasn't waiting anymore.

Dana stopped just off the porch, her arms crossing tight over her chest as she stared out toward the tree line. The wind had picked up, but the trees weren't swaying right. It was too controlled, too synchronized.

Like they were watching.

Ben didn't say anything at first. He had seen enough of her over the years to know when she needed a second.

Dana exhaled, trying to steady her pulse. She hadn't realized how much she had been holding in until now.

Her mother was right.

Miriam was right.

And that meant that whatever had happened to Morgan—whatever had been lurking in the corners of this town for generations—was real.

She felt the first flicker of genuine fear. Not just unease, not just grief—but fear.

And worse—they knew she knew.

Ben finally broke the silence. "You alright?"

Dana closed her eyes briefly, then forced herself to nod. "Yeah."

It wasn't true.

But it was enough for now.

She turned toward the car, gripping the strap of her bag tighter. She could feel the weight of the book pressing against her side.

It felt like a responsibility she hadn't asked for.

She glanced back once—just once—at Miriam's house.

The old woman was still at the window, watching.

And though her expression was unreadable, Dana could have sworn she saw something like regret.

Chapter 4

The sky had dimmed to deep blue, the sun sinking lower but not gone yet. The stretch of road ahead was lined with towering pines, their silhouettes sharpening against the fading light.

Dana sat stiffly in the passenger seat, staring out the window, but not really seeing anything. Her thoughts churned, tangled with half-formed questions and fragmented memories she still couldn't quite grasp.

The book Miriam had given her rested heavy against her thigh, its presence as impossible to ignore as the dull ache growing at the base of her skull.

She should have felt relieved to finally have answers—or at least a path toward them. But instead, her mind spun in restless loops.

Morgan's jacket. The missing memories. The feeling of something watching.

And now Miriam's warning.

"If you keep digging, they will come back for you."

Dana exhaled sharply and rubbed at her temple. They were already here.

Ben glanced at her from the driver's seat. He hadn't said much since they left Miriam's house, but Dana could feel him watching. Waiting.

"You gonna say something?" he asked finally. His tone was light, but there was an edge to it.

Dana kept her eyes on the dimming road ahead. "What do you want me to say?"

"That you're not about to spiral."

Dana snorted. "Last time I spiraled, you got laid."

Ben coughed, nearly jerking the wheel. "Jesus, Dana."

Dana smirked at Ben's discomfort, but the amusement was fleeting, hollow. The moment lingered between them, the joke hanging in the air longer than it should have.

Because it wasn't just a joke.

Because that night hadn't just been some drunken mistake—not really.

It had been months after her mother's first hospital stay, when the weight of waiting for the inevitable had made her feel suffocated, desperate to forget, desperate to feel anything but the goddamn dread.

Ben had been the only one who hadn't treated her like she was breaking.

And maybe that was why, after too much whiskey and too little sleep, she had let herself spiral. Right into his arms, right into a night that had been too rough, too desperate, too full of everything she wasn't supposed to need.

And the worst part?

She hadn't regretted it.

Not until the morning after, when neither of them had said a damn word about it.

She blinked back to the present, rubbing her fingers against the seam of her jeans. The book pressed against her thigh like an anchor, keeping her from sinking too far into the past.

Ben was still staring straight ahead, jaw tight, like he knew exactly what she was thinking but wasn't about to open that door.

She let out a slow breath. "Don't worry, Sheriff. Your reputation is intact."

He let out a short, dry laugh. "Yeah, that's what I'm worried about."

Dana shook her head, looking back toward the window. The sky had darkened another shade, the trees blurring together as the road curved ahead.

The weight in her chest hadn't lifted.

If anything, it had settled in deeper.

Dana let the silence stretch between them again. Normally, she wouldn't mind it. Normally, she liked the way Ben didn't force conversations the way other people did. But tonight, the quiet was too thick.

Too much like the spaces in her memories that had been hollowed out.

Her grip tightened on her jeans. "Ben."

He flicked his gaze toward her. "Yeah?"

She swallowed. "What if I didn't see everything that night?"

Ben's eyes flickered toward her, but he didn't speak yet.

Dana exhaled sharply. "The night Morgan disappeared."

Just saying it out loud made her skin prickle, like invoking it gave it weight again.

"I told the police everything I knew," she continued. "Morgan ran ahead of me into the woods, I followed her voice, and then—" She frowned, her thoughts stuttering like a film reel missing frames.

Then what?

She had always told the story the same way. That she had heard Morgan scream, that she had reached the clearing only seconds too late, and Morgan was gone.

But now, with everything Miriam had said—**everything Dana was starting to remember**—she realized there was something wrong with that memory.

It wasn't seconds.

It was longer.

An empty space, a void in her memory where time should have been.

And she hadn't questioned it. Not once.

Ben didn't speak right away, and that was almost worse than if he had brushed it off.

He exhaled through his nose. "What did Miriam say?"

Dana chewed the inside of her cheek. "That they take pieces of people."

Ben's jaw flexed, but he didn't look at her. His focus stayed straight ahead, eyes scanning the road, like he was processing it carefully before giving it space to be real.

"Then I guess we need to figure out what piece they took from you."

Dana's fingers twitched in her lap. The weight of Ben's words settled into her chest, heavy, unshakable.

What piece had they taken?

The question shouldn't have made sense, but it did. Deep down, in a way she couldn't articulate, she knew something had been taken from her that night. She just didn't know what.

The hollowed-out space in her memory wasn't natural. It wasn't trauma blocking it out, or grief twisting events.

It was a wound.

And wounds left scars.

Ben's grip on the wheel tightened. "You're sure you didn't black out?"

Dana scoffed, but there wasn't much humor behind it. "I wasn't drunk, Ben."

"That's not what I meant," he muttered. "I mean—if you lost time that night, wouldn't you have noticed? Wouldn't you have felt it?"

Dana swallowed. Would she?

For all these years, she had assumed her memory was whole. That what she remembered was the truth. That Morgan had simply vanished, slipping through reality in a way that didn't make sense, but that Dana had at least witnessed the moment it happened.

But now?

Now she wasn't so sure.

She turned her gaze toward the window again, watching the trees blur past in the twilight.

A flicker.

Not in the present—in her mind.

Morgan's laughter. The scent of pine needles and damp earth. A branch snapping too far away.

The wrongness that crept in before the silence.

The moment between the scream and the empty space in her mind.

Dana sucked in a sharp breath. There was something there.

Something she had forgotten.

Something she wasn't supposed to remember.

Her nails dug into her palms. Not now. She wasn't ready for this—not here, not yet.

She forced herself to exhale, steadying her pulse.

Ben glanced at her again, picking up on the shift. "Dana."

"I'm fine," she said, too fast.

Ben's brow furrowed, but he didn't push. Not yet.

Instead, he tapped his fingers against the steering wheel, shifting the subject. "We should figure out our next move."

Dana hesitated, still half-tangled in the edges of her missing memory. "What do you have in mind?"

Ben sighed. "Well, we've got a few options." His voice was measured, focused—trying to bring her back to the present.

"We can go through that book Miriam gave you—see if anything in there matches up with the disappearances. Or—" He paused, jaw tightening. "Or we can talk to someone else who might remember more than they let on."

Dana frowned. "Who?"

Ben hesitated. Then—"Morgan's parents."

Dana's stomach twisted.

Morgan's parents.

She hadn't spoken to them in years. Not since the early days after the disappearance, when their house had become a second home for police officers and reporters, when Mrs. Reece's face had hollowed out from grief, and Mr. Reece had stopped speaking entirely.

She remembered the last time she had seen them—how their eyes had searched her face, looking for answers she didn't have. Looking for a truth she couldn't give them.

She shook her head. "No."

Ben glanced at her. "Dana—"

"No," she repeated, sharper this time. "I'm not dragging them back into this."

Ben exhaled through his nose. Not frustrated. Not surprised.

"They were already dragged into it, Dana. Fifteen years ago."

Dana knew that. But it wasn't the same.

"They lost their daughter," she said, voice tight. "And if we start asking questions now—if we make them relive that night—what do you think that's going to do to them?"

Ben kept his eyes on the road, but she could feel the weight of his words before he even spoke them.

"What if it helps them?"

Dana let out a sharp laugh, but there was no humor in it. "Yeah? You really think dredging up a sixteen-year-old mystery is going to give them closure? You think they want to hear that their daughter wasn't just missing, but taken?"

The word hung in the car, sharp as a blade.

Taken.

It was the first time she had said it aloud.

Ben didn't answer right away.

He let the word sit between them, let Dana feel it, let her hear the truth in it.

And the worst part?

She couldn't take it back.

Ben's fingers drummed once against the steering wheel. "I think they deserve the choice," he said. "And I think if it were your kid, you'd want to know."

Dana clenched her jaw, staring hard out the window. The trees had darkened now, the last traces of sun giving way to deep blue shadows.

It didn't matter what she wanted.

It didn't matter what Morgan's parents wanted.

The truth was coming for them whether they were ready for it or not.

She exhaled, long and slow. "Give me a night."

Ben raised a brow. "To do what?"

"To read." Dana glanced down at the book resting against her leg. "To see what the hell we're actually dealing with before we bring anyone else into this."

Ben didn't argue.

He just nodded. "Alright."

And the road stretched on, dark and endless ahead of them.

Ben pulled into the driveway of the motel just outside town, its flickering neon vacancy sign buzzing against the deep blue twilight. The place wasn't much—just a handful of rooms, a peeling green awning over the front office, and a single streetlamp that barely lit the parking lot.

It wasn't home.

But it wasn't her mother's house either.

Dana exhaled, stretching her stiff legs as she stepped out of the car. The weight of the book was still pressed against her thigh, and she found herself gripping it tighter than she meant to.

Ben grabbed their bags from the trunk, his movements quiet, deliberate. He knew Dana needed space, and for once, he wasn't pushing her to talk.

Fine by her.

She just wanted to read.

Inside the room, the air was cool and stale, like the place hadn't been aired out in weeks. The bedspread was an ugly shade of mustard yellow, the carpet thin, the single lamp casting a dim glow over the worn wooden desk in the corner.

Dana dropped into the chair, setting the book down in front of her.

It looked older in this light. The leather was cracked, the edges frayed, and there was no title, no author. Just a dark cover, smooth except for the faint impression of a symbol she didn't recognize.

Ben tossed his bag onto the other bed, rolling his shoulders before eyeing her. "You sure you don't want me to stick around for this?"

Dana flicked the cover open. "I need to do this alone."

Ben studied her for a beat, then nodded once. "I'll be next door."

The door clicked shut behind him, and Dana let out a breath.

Finally.

She turned the first page.

The handwriting was small and dense, the ink faded in places but still readable.

The first line made her pulse skip.

"The ones who vanish are not truly lost. They are taken."

Dana's mouth went dry.

She forced herself to keep reading, her eyes scanning the deliberate, almost frantic script.

"They do not kill. They do not steal bodies. They take something deeper—something that cannot be seen, cannot be touched. And in doing so, they erase something vital, something that leaves only the shell behind."

Her stomach turned.

She turned the page, fingers pressing harder into the fragile paper.

Dana took a deep breath as the words on the page stared back at her, sharp and damning.

"You do not see them until they want you to see them. You do not hear them until they whisper your name. And by then, it is already too late."

A cold shiver snaked down her spine.

Because she had heard it.

At Miriam's house. Soft, distant. A voice she had ignored, let fester unspoken.

But she had heard it.

Dana swallowed, forcing herself to breathe, to move, to turn the page—

The door swung open.

She nearly jumped out of her skin.

Ben stood in the doorway, expression neutral, posture relaxed, as if he hadn't just shaved a year off her life.

"Forgot my keys."

Dana exhaled sharply, closing the book with a little more force than necessary. "You have the worst timing, you know that?"

Ben stepped inside, grabbing the keys off the nightstand where he'd tossed them earlier. His gaze flicked to her face, then to the book, taking in the way her shoulders were still rigid, tense.

He didn't ask what she'd read. Not yet.

Instead, he nodded toward the book. "You find something?"

Dana ran her fingers along the edge of the leather cover, hesitant. "Yeah." Her voice was quieter now. "I think so."

Ben lingered in the doorway a moment longer, then sighed and nodded toward the connecting wall between their rooms. "If you start talking in your sleep, keep it down."

Dana smirked faintly, though the weight in her chest hadn't lifted. "Yeah. Sure."

Ben pulled the door shut behind him.

She stared at the book in front of her.

The room felt colder now.

And the words she had read wouldn't leave her mind.

Chapter 5

Dana woke to the dull gray light of early morning filtering through the thin motel curtains. The room was too quiet, the kind of quiet that felt deliberate. It was like something had been listening all night and was waiting for her to wake up.

She exhaled, rolling onto her back and staring at the ceiling. She didn't remember falling asleep. The last thing she remembered was the book, its weight in her lap, and the words crawling under her skin. She had read until her eyes blurred, until exhaustion dragged her under.

And somehow, despite everything, she hadn't woken up once.

Small victories.

Dana swung her legs over the side of the bed, rubbing the stiffness from her neck, before glancing at the clock. It was 7:13 AM.

Outside, she could hear faint movement in the next room—Ben, probably getting ready. At least he'd let her sleep.

She smirked faintly, running a hand through her hair. "No late-night visits this time," she muttered.

Fifteen minutes later, she stepped outside, the morning air cool and crisp, the scent of damp asphalt still clinging from the night's rain. Ben was already by the car, a steaming cup of coffee in one hand, a paper bag in the other.

"Figured you'd need caffeine," he said, holding out the cup as she approached.

Dana took it, sighing in appreciation as the warmth seeped into her fingers. "You're getting soft."

Ben arched a brow. "You're just figuring that out?"

She took a sip, relishing the bitter kick, then nodded toward the bag. "That for me, too, or did you already eat half the bagels?"

Ben handed it over without argument, watching as she leaned against the car's hood. "So," he said, "what's the verdict? That book of yours give you anything we can actually use?"

Dana hesitated, fingers tightening around the cup. The words from last night still sat heavy in her head.

She glanced at him. "Depends. You believe in things that watch from the dark?"

Ben's jaw ticked. "I believe something's been watching you for a long time."

Dana eyed the tree line for a moment longer, her pulse steady but too aware of how exposed they were standing out in the open. She turned back to Ben.

"Let's get out of here."

Ben frowned. "Where?"

"Someplace normal," she muttered, grabbing her coffee off the hood of the car. "Someplace that doesn't feel like something's waiting for us to look away."

Ben didn't argue. He just nodded, tossing his bag into the back seat before climbing behind the wheel.

Fifteen minutes later, they pulled into the small, familiar coffee shop on the edge of town—the kind of place that hadn't changed in decades. The sign out front still flickered at the edges; the glass windows were covered with old posters for local events, and inside, the scent of roasted coffee and warm cinnamon wrapped around her like something safe, something untouched by whatever else was creeping through this town.

Dana exhaled slowly as they stepped inside. The quiet murmur of conversation, the clink of mugs against saucers, the faint hum of an old radio playing in the background was grounding.

It was normal.

And for the first time since she'd come back to Pine Hollow, Dana needed normal.

They settled into a corner booth, the seat cushions cracked from years of use, the wood table polished smooth by time and habit. Ben ordered for them—black coffee for him, something strong but sweet for her.

Dana curled her fingers around the paper coffee cup when it arrived, letting the heat sink into her palms. For a moment, neither of them spoke.

Ben let her take her time.

Finally, Dana exhaled and set the book down between them.

"I read a lot last night," she admitted.

Ben nodded, waiting.

She hesitated, choosing her words carefully. "That book… it isn't just a collection of local disappearances. It's more than that. It's a record of people who were taken—of people who weren't meant to be remembered."

Ben's expression didn't change, but he sat up a little straighter. "What do you mean?"

Dana ran her fingers along the book's spine. "I mean… the ones who vanish? They don't just disappear." She swallowed. "They're erased."

Ben's fingers tapped against his mug, thoughtful. "Erased how?"

Dana hesitated. "Not physically. Not completely. But the longer they're gone, the harder it is for people to remember them. Like a dream that fades the moment you wake up."

Ben frowned. "People don't just forget other people exist."

Dana looked up at him, eyes shadowed. "What if they do?"

Ben didn't respond immediately. She could tell he was trying to piece it together, to make it fit inside a world that still had rules.

Finally, he exhaled, shaking his head. "That's why your mother was afraid."

Dana nodded, voice quieter now. "She was trying to protect me from forgetting."

She hesitated, fingers tightening around her mug.

"And now that I'm remembering…"

She didn't have to finish the sentence.

They both knew what came next.

Dana took a slow sip of her coffee, trying to anchor herself in the moment. The normalcy of the café, the warmth of the cup in her hands, the quiet murmur of conversation—it should have felt safe.

It didn't.

Because no matter how much she tried to ground herself, she couldn't shake the feeling that they weren't alone.

Not really.

Ben watched her, quiet but alert, waiting. She could tell he was still processing everything she'd told him—everything she'd read.

"People who vanish don't just disappear," she repeated, voice lower now. "They get erased. Slowly, piece by piece, until nothing's left."

Ben's jaw ticked, and she saw the moment it truly sank in.

"That means," he said, "if we're not careful—"

"You and I could end up the same way."

The words settled between them like a weight, and for a moment, neither of them spoke.

Outside, the wind shifted.

And something changed.

It was small at first.

A shift in the sound of the café.

The low hum of conversation dulled like someone had turned the volume down just a notch. Not enough to be obvious, but enough that Dana felt it.

Then, the air grew colder.

Not a sudden draft, not a breeze from the door opening. Just… a chill creeping in from nowhere, crawling over her skin like the first touch of winter.

Ben must have felt it too because his fingers tightened around his mug, his shoulders going tense.

Dana exhaled through her nose and forced herself to look.

The café looked the same. The same counter, the same pastries in the glass case, the same barista wiping down a table near the window.

But something was off.

Her gaze swept over the tables, over the handful of people sitting inside—people who had been there when they walked in.

Except…

Had that man in the far booth been there before?

Had that woman by the window always had her back turned?

Dana's stomach clenched.

She couldn't remember.

And the longer she looked, the less certain she became.

She turned back to Ben, her voice quiet. "We need to go."

Ben was already standing. He dropped some cash on the table, grabbed the book, and followed her toward the door without hesitation.

They stepped out into the morning light, and the moment the café door swung shut behind them—

The weight lifted.

The cold was gone.

The sound returned to normal.

Dana turned, glancing back through the window. The café looked the same. No strange figures, no eerie silence.

But deep in her gut, she knew.

Something inside that café had been watching.

And it had almost made her forget.

They walked in silence back to the car. Not a comfortable silence, not the kind they usually shared—this one was weighted, thick with the unspoken.

Dana reached for the door handle, then hesitated.

She turned, looking back at the café, at the people inside.

Try to remember.

Her jaw tightened as she scanned the tables, the barista behind the counter, the man in the far booth.

Had he been drinking coffee? Eating something? Was he even there when they walked in?

Dana's stomach twisted. She had no idea.

She could picture the café as a whole—the general layout, the sound of the coffee machines, the scent of cinnamon and espresso.

But the details?

They were already slipping.

Ben must have noticed her hesitation because he shifted beside her. "Dana."

She swallowed and turned to him. "Do you remember the barista's name?"

Ben blinked, caught off guard. "What?"

"The barista," she repeated, pulse picking up. "The one who made our coffee. Did they wear a name tag? Did they say their name?"

Ben didn't answer right away.

He glanced back at the café window, his brow furrowed, the muscle in his jaw ticking like he was trying to force something into place that wouldn't quite fit.

Dana watched him, waiting, her pulse steady but too aware of how much time was passing.

The seconds stretched.

Ben rubbed a hand over his mouth, exhaled sharply. "I mean, I—I must've seen their name. They always wear tags at places like this." He shook his head, like that would knock something loose. "I just... I wasn't paying attention."

Dana didn't respond.

Because she knew it wasn't true.

She had ordered from them. She had taken her coffee directly from their hands. And yet—

Nothing.

No name, no face that made sense in her memory.

Just a blur, a presence that should have been there but was already slipping away.

Ben ran a hand through his hair, glancing down at his coffee cup as if it might hold an answer. "Alright," he muttered, forcing a breath. "Alright. Say you're right. Say we don't remember because—because something in there wasn't real."

Dana's grip tightened around her own cup. "You feel it, don't you?"

He hesitated.

Then—a slow, reluctant nod.

Dana exhaled, looking back at the café one last time. It looked so damn normal—warm light, quiet conversations, people sipping their drinks.

But she knew better now.

Just because something looked familiar didn't mean it belonged.

She opened the car door and slid inside. Ben followed, his movements slower, more measured. He was still working through it, still grappling with the gaps.

The moment he started the car, the radio clicked on.

Static.

A soft, whispering hum beneath the white noise.

Ben didn't react at first, like his brain hadn't quite registered it.

Then, as the static deepened, something slipped through.

A voice—garbled, distant, like something trying to push through a bad connection.

Only two words came through clearly.

"Come back."

Ben stilled.

Dana swallowed hard and turned off the radio.

Neither of them spoke.

But they both understood what it meant.

Something in that café had noticed them.

And it wasn't finished yet.

The silence in the car stretched too long.

Dana's fingers curled around her coffee cup, her grip just a little too tight. The words on the radio still echoed in her mind.

Come back.

Ben exhaled sharply through his nose, like he was shaking something off. Then, he turned the key in the ignition again, the engine rumbling to life. "Old frequencies pick up weird interference sometimes," he muttered. "Could've been anything."

Dana didn't believe that.

But she didn't call him on it.

Not yet.

She nodded, feigning agreement, taking a slow sip of coffee. "Yeah," she murmured. "Probably."

Ben pulled onto the road, eyes steady ahead. His posture was relaxed—too relaxed. Like he was forcing it.

Dana studied him for a beat. He had heard it, too. She knew he had.

But he wasn't ready to admit it.

Or maybe he was just hoping that if he didn't acknowledge it, it wouldn't be real.

Dana turned toward the window, watching the trees blur past.

She didn't trust her own memory anymore.

The book had said people who vanished weren't just taken. They were erased.

How long before she forgot something else? Before another piece of reality slipped through the cracks?

She swallowed hard, pressing her fingernails into the cardboard of her coffee cup to anchor herself.

"I think we should talk to Morgan's parents," Ben said suddenly, breaking the quiet.

Dana forced herself to blink, to focus, to push away the creeping fog in her head.

Dana exhaled slowly, keeping her gaze on the trees blurring past the window. She had known this moment was coming—the inevitable next step.

Morgan's parents.

Revisiting them meant revisiting everything. The police interviews, the hopeless searches, the way Mrs. Reece had gripped Dana's hands so tightly her nails had left marks, begging her to tell them something, anything.

And worst of all?

The look in Mr. Reece's eyes.

Empty.

Not with grief. With something worse.

Like a man who knew something had been stolen from him but couldn't name what.

Dana swallowed, fingers pressing against the paper coffee cup. "I don't know if that's a good idea."

Ben's hands stayed steady on the wheel, but he flicked a glance toward her. "You're the one who wanted to keep remembering. You think they don't deserve that chance too?"

Dana let out a breath, shaking her head. "It's not that simple."

"Seems simple to me."

"It's not." Her voice was sharper than she meant, and she saw Ben register it. She sighed, softening slightly. "What if we bring this to them, and it just… wrecks them all over again? What if they've spent years forcing themselves to forget?"

Ben didn't respond right away.

Dana rubbed at her temple. "And what if they don't even remember her?"

That was the real fear.

Not that they'd be devastated. That they'd be empty. That when Dana said Morgan's name, they'd pause, hesitate, frown like they weren't sure who she was talking about.

Ben exhaled, tapping his fingers against the steering wheel in thought.

"They might not remember her," he admitted. "But if they do, and we don't ask—"

He let the thought hang.

Dana sighed. He was right.

She hated that he was right.

"Fine," she muttered. "We'll talk to them."

Ben nodded, like he'd already known she'd get there eventually. "Good."

Dana pressed her lips together, forcing down the unease creeping up her spine.

Some doors, once opened, couldn't be closed again.

And this was one of them.

The drive to the Reece house was too quiet.

Dana kept her eyes on the road ahead, but her mind was already miles behind. Memory was a fragile thing—she knew that now.

But grief?

Grief dug trenches. Grief carved itself into places that time couldn't touch.

And if Morgan's parents still remembered her…

Then grief was all that would be waiting for them inside that house.

The Reece house sat at the end of a long, cracked driveway, tucked behind trees that had grown taller than Dana remembered.

The place was almost exactly the same. The same dull gray siding, the same crooked mailbox, the same wind chime hanging by the porch that never seemed to move, no matter how strong the wind blew.

But something was different.

The grass was overgrown, the paint more faded, the windows too still.

A house like this should have felt empty. It didn't.

It felt like something inside it was waiting.

Ben pulled up beside the curb, cutting the engine. The ticking of the cooling car filled the silence between them.

Dana swallowed hard, gripping her cup as if the warmth could ground her. "Last chance to back out."

Ben huffed. "Not happening."

Dana exhaled sharply, forcing herself to open the door. "Didn't think so."

They stepped onto the porch, and Dana's stomach twisted.

The wind chime remained perfectly still.

She raised a hand to knock—

The door opened before she could.

Mrs. Reece stood there.

She looked older, smaller than Dana remembered, but her eyes were still sharp, blue, knowing.

For a split second, Dana braced herself.

Would she recognize her?

Would she remember why they were here?

Then—a flicker of something in her expression.

Recognition.

"Dana?" Mrs. Reece's voice was soft, uncertain—but real.

Dana let out a breath she hadn't realized she was holding.

She remembered.

Mrs. Reece hesitated in the doorway, her fingers tightening on the edge of the frame. For a moment, Dana thought she might turn them away.

But then, the tension in her shoulders eased, and she stepped back. "Come in."

Dana swallowed the lump in her throat and stepped inside, Ben close behind her.

The house smelled the same—wood polish, old books, the faintest trace of lavender. But underneath it, there was something else.

Something stale.

Like a house full of words that hadn't been spoken in a very long time.

Mrs. Reece led them to the living room, where the furniture sat exactly as Dana remembered. The same overstuffed couch, the lace doilies on the arms of the chairs, the family photos lining the mantle.

But something was wrong.

Dana's gaze flickered over the frames. The Reeces had always been the kind of family who filled their home with pictures—vacations, birthdays, holidays, Morgan's school portraits.

But now…

Now there were gaps.

Some frames were missing. Others had been turned face-down.

Dana's stomach twisted. Had they removed Morgan's photos on purpose? Or had something else erased them?

Mrs. Reece lowered herself onto the couch, smoothing invisible wrinkles from her slacks. "It's been a long time," she murmured.

Dana nodded, unable to make her voice work right away.

Ben, always the one to fill silence, cleared his throat. "Thank you for seeing us, Mrs. Reece."

She gave him a small, tired smile. "I remember you. You used to come around with the other boys, back when…" She trailed off, shaking her head, like she had almost said something she wasn't supposed to.

Dana shifted forward on the armchair, resting her elbows on her knees. "Mrs. Reece… we came because we're trying to understand what happened to your daughter."

Mrs. Reece sat very still, her hands folded in her lap. Her eyes flickered toward the turned-down photo frames on the mantle, then back to Dana.

She frowned slightly, like someone trying to recall a dream that had already begun to slip away.

"I… had a daughter," she said slowly. Her voice was steady, but there was hesitation beneath it.

Dana felt her pulse skip.

Mrs. Reece pressed her lips together, searching for something. A detail. A face. A name.

But whatever she was looking for, it wasn't coming.

"I remember…" She let out a breath, shaking her head. "I remember loving her. I remember being… proud."

She swallowed, her fingers curling against the fabric of her slacks. "But—" She hesitated. "I can't seem to… picture her."

Dana felt something inside her lurch.

Because this wasn't just grief fogging a mother's memory.

This was erasure.

And it was winning.

Ben shifted beside Dana, his jaw tight. He said nothing, but Dana could feel him watching, waiting, as if he was gauging how far this would go.

Dana leaned forward slightly. "Do you remember her name?"

Mrs. Reece blinked. She hesitated.

And for a moment—too long a moment—it was clear she didn't know.

Then, barely above a whisper—

"Morgan."

Dana's throat tightened.

Mrs. Reece exhaled sharply, pressing a hand against her forehead. "I—yes. Of course. Morgan." She forced a weak smile. "How could I forget?"

Dana and Ben exchanged a glance.

She had almost forgotten.

And Dana knew—if they had waited any longer, she would have.

Mrs. Reece's hand still rested against her forehead, her breathing shallow. Dana could see the strain in her features—the way her mind was grasping for pieces of something that wasn't there anymore.

Then—a sound.

A soft, distant creak.

Dana turned her head sharply toward the hallway.

The house had been silent since they arrived. But now, the air felt different—charged, too still in some places and shifting in others, like the walls themselves had noticed them.

And then, footsteps.

Slow, deliberate.

A shadow moved at the end of the hallway, and Mr. Reece stepped into view.

Dana's stomach tightened.

Mr. Reece had always been a quiet man, reserved even before Morgan disappeared. But as he stepped forward now, there was something off about him.

His expression was calm. Too calm.

His eyes—they weren't empty.

They were watching.

Dana's fingers dug into her jeans. She had been prepared for grief, for confusion. But this?

This felt like recognition.

Like he knew why they were here.

Like he had been waiting for them.

Ben sat up straighter beside her, shifting his weight. "Mr. Reece," he said, voice even.

The older man nodded slightly, stepping further into the room. "Sheriff." His gaze flickered to Dana. "Dana."

Her name felt strange in his mouth. Not unfamiliar—too deliberate.

"You're looking for something," he said. Not a question. A statement.

Dana's pulse picked up. The air in the room grew heavier.

She swallowed. "We just want to understand what happened."

Mr. Reece stared at her. And then, he smiled.

It was small. Subtle. Wrong.

"You already do."

Dana's blood ran cold.

Mr. Reece's words lingered in the air, thick and deliberate.

"You already do."

There was no confusion in his voice, no struggle to remember—just certainty.

Something inside Dana screamed at her to move, to say something, to break the moment before it could take hold of her too.

But before she could, Mrs. Reece spoke first.

"David?"

Her voice was soft, uncertain—but laced with something Dana hadn't heard from her before. Fear.

She shifted forward on the couch, staring at her husband like she was looking at a stranger.

"David, what are you talking about?"

Mr. Reece's expression didn't change at first.

But then—a flicker.

Something passed through his eyes, something brief but violent—a crack in the stillness of his face, like a ripple disturbing deep water.

His jaw twitched.

And then, it was gone.

Just like that.

He blinked, brow furrowing as if he had just woken up from a long sleep. His gaze darted between Dana, Ben, and his wife, confusion settling into his features.

"I—" He exhaled, rubbing a hand over his face. "What were we talking about?"

Mrs. Reece swallowed. "You... you just said they already knew what happened."

Mr. Reece frowned, looking genuinely lost. He let out a short, nervous chuckle. "No, I—I don't think I did."

Dana's grip on her thigh tightened. She knew what she heard.

And she was willing to bet Ben had heard it too.

But now, looking at him, Mr. Reece was just himself again.

The air in the room shifted back to something normal.

And yet—Dana couldn't shake the feeling that for a moment, something else had been here.

And it had used Mr. Reece to speak.

The room stayed heavy with the weight of what wasn't being said.

Dana knew she should press further. Knew she should ask more—push for something, anything that might still be buried under whatever had hollowed out their memories.

But she could already see it in Mrs. Reece's eyes.

There was nothing left.

Whatever had taken Morgan hadn't just stolen her away. It had stolen the very idea of her.

Ben exhaled, then stood, all business now. "I think that's enough for today."

Mrs. Reece blinked, as if coming out of a daze. Mr. Reece rubbed his hands over his knees, looking at Ben like he wasn't sure when he had even sat down.

"Right," Mr. Reece murmured, offering a small, polite smile. "Of course."

Dana didn't move right away.

There was a sinking, hollow feeling in her chest. Like she had come expecting to find something half-buried, half-intact.

Instead, there was nothing at all.

She had wanted answers.

And all she had found was a grave where memory used to be.

Mrs. Reece stood and walked them to the door, her movements mechanical. There was no anger, no discomfort—just a quiet, passive politeness.

As if they had come to visit for no reason at all.

Dana hesitated at the threshold, glancing back one last time at the family photos on the mantle. The gaps. The empty spaces.

If she hadn't known better, she might have thought the missing pictures had just fallen, broken, never replaced.

But she did know better.

Something had taken Morgan.

And it had never intended to leave a trace.

Mrs. Reece offered a soft, distant smile. "Drive safe."

Dana forced herself to nod, stepping out into the fading light.

Behind her, the door closed without a sound.

The car felt too quiet as Dana shut the door behind her.

She stared straight ahead, hands resting on her thighs, pulse still too fast. The Reeces had been polite, kind, normal—but there was something terribly wrong about it.

Because they had forgotten Morgan so completely that they didn't even know they had forgotten.

Ben exhaled sharply and ran a hand over his jaw. "Jesus."

Dana turned to him. "You felt it too."

He let out a humorless laugh, gripping the wheel but not starting the car yet. "Yeah. Yeah, I felt it." He shook his head. "That was—God, Dana, that was worse than if they'd been angry. Worse than if they'd yelled at us to leave."

Dana swallowed. "Because there was nothing left."

Ben nodded, jaw tight. "Nothing. Like she was never there."

A silence stretched between them, but it wasn't empty.

It was thick. Heavy with realization.

Dana flexed her fingers, trying to shake the lingering numbness from them. "She was their daughter, Ben. And they don't even feel like they lost her. They don't feel anything at all."

Ben clenched his jaw. "That's not natural."

Dana exhaled, staring out the windshield. The house sat behind them, perfectly still.

It had been a home once. Now it was just a place where a family had lived, past tense.

A place that didn't remember its own missing pieces.

Ben finally started the car.

Neither of them spoke as they pulled away.

Because there was nothing left to say.

The ride back was quieter than Dana expected.

Not in the heavy, suffocating way that had settled over them after leaving the Reece house—but in a way that felt like a pause between chapters.

Like they both needed a minute to process.

The records office had been a bust—closing just as they arrived. A locked door, drawn blinds, a sign on the door that read "Closed at 4 PM" like some kind of cruel joke.

Now, back at the motel, they had nothing left to do but go over what they knew.

And what they knew?

Wasn't much.

Dana kicked off her boots the second she stepped into the room, flopping onto the chair by the desk with a sigh. "Alright. Let's lay it out."

Ben shrugged off his jacket, tossing it over the back of the chair across from her. "We know the Reeces don't remember Morgan. Not in any real way."

Dana nodded, stretching out her legs. "And we know my mom was trying to keep me from forgetting, too."

Ben leaned forward, elbows on his knees. "Which means whatever this is—it doesn't just take people. It takes their memory."

Dana's stomach twisted. She hated hearing it said out loud.

But it was the truth.

And they were getting closer to it.

She ran a hand through her hair, exhaling slowly. "So. What now?"

Ben leaned back, studying her. "We drink?"

Dana snorted. "Not exactly the investigative approach I had in mind."

"Why not?" He smirked, shaking his head. "We're hitting dead ends. Might as well celebrate what little progress we made."

Dana rolled her eyes but didn't argue when he reached into his bag and pulled out a bottle of whiskey.

She raised a brow. "Really? Just carrying that around?"

Ben shrugged, twisting off the cap. "I come prepared."

Dana snatched the bottle before he could pour himself a drink, taking a sip straight from it. The burn settled low in her stomach, warm and familiar.

Ben watched her, eyes flickering to her lips just a second too long.

Something shifted.

The air between them stretched, pulled tight.

Dana smirked, handing the bottle back. "You staring at something, Sheriff?"

Ben took the bottle, his expression unreadable. "Noticed you got a little more relaxed all of a sudden."

"Yeah, well." She leaned back in the chair, tipping her head against the cushion. "Maybe I needed it."

Ben took a slow sip, watching her over the rim of the bottle. "Guess we both did."

The weight in the room changed.

Not in a bad way.

Not in the way it had back at the Reece house, or in the café, or any of the places where something had been watching.

This was different.

This was familiar.

This was that night, all over again.

And Dana knew Ben felt it, too.

She shifted in her seat, stretching her legs out, toe nudging against his boot. "Careful, Sheriff."

Ben's lips quirked at the corner. "Of what?"

Dana tilted her head slightly, watching him. "You tell me."

And then—the lights flickered.

Once.

Twice.

Then—out.

The room plunged into darkness.

And just beyond the window—something knocked.

The knock came again.

Sharp. Deliberate.

Dana's breath caught in her throat.

She didn't move.

Ben was already on his feet, the whiskey bottle forgotten on the table. His hand hovered near his holster—not quite drawing his gun yet, but close.

The motel room was pitch black, save for the faint glow of the parking lot light seeping through the curtains.

But outside the window?

There was nothing.

No shadow, no movement.

Just the sound of knuckles against glass.

Knock. Knock. Knock.

Louder this time. Rhythmic. Insistent.

Ben took a slow step toward the window, his body tense. "Who's there?"

The knocking stopped.

Dana swallowed, her pulse hammering in her ears. The air in the room had changed. Not just from the darkness—but from something else.

Something wrong.

Then—

The entire window rattled.

A frantic, violent pounding. Not a knock. Not anymore.

Dana shot to her feet. "Ben—"

The pounding stopped.

Silence.

Heavy. Suffocating.

Dana's breath came shallow, her skin prickling with a sensation she couldn't name. She glanced at Ben, whose grip on his gun had tightened.

Then—

The doorknob twisted.

The sound was gentle. Almost casual.

The way someone might check if a door was unlocked.

Dana's stomach lurched.

Ben took a slow step forward, angling himself toward the door. He didn't speak. Didn't call out this time.

Dana's heart slammed against her ribs as the knob rattled again—harder this time.

The door held.

And then—

Silence.

A long, unbearable stretch of nothing.

Then the light flickered back on.

The room looked the same. The window was closed. The door was locked.

But Dana knew—something had been here.

And it had wanted in.

The silence after the light returned was the worst part.

Like the room itself was holding its breath.

Ben glanced at Dana, his expression unreadable, but she could see the decision settling in his eyes before he even spoke.

"I'm going out."

Dana's stomach tightened.

"Ben—"

But he was already moving, reaching for the door, gun drawn but low, cautious. His stance was controlled, practiced. He had done this a hundred times before.

This time was different.

Dana felt it deep in her chest.

"Stay here," he murmured.

Dana's throat went dry. "I don't think you should—"

Ben shot her a look. "We can't just sit here, Dana."

She gasped. *Yes, we can.*

Because every nerve in her body was screaming at her that if he walked out that door, something was waiting for him.

And it wouldn't let him come back.

"Ben."

But he was already stepping outside.

And Dana?

She didn't follow.

Because something—some awful, unshakable force—was telling her that if she stepped over that threshold, she wouldn't come back either.

The door clicked shut behind him.

The seconds stretched.

Dana forced herself to count them.

One.

Two.

Three.

A soft crunch outside—gravel shifting under his boots.

Four.

Five.

Nothing.

She swallowed hard, taking slow, steady breaths. He was being careful. He was checking the perimeter. He was coming back.

Six.

Seven.

Eight.

Still nothing.

Dana squeezed her hands into fists, her fingernails digging into her palms. The air felt thick, pressing in on her.

Nine.

Ten.

And then—

The motel room door swung open into the night air.

Dana stumbled forward, breath caught in her throat.

The parking lot stretched before her, empty.

Too empty.

Because where the cruiser had been parked just seconds ago—

There was nothing.

No car. No footprints. No sign that Ben had ever been there.

Dana's heart pounded, a sharp, painful rhythm against her ribs.

This wasn't possible.

She had heard him step outside. She had counted his footsteps.

And now?

Now there was just an empty space where the car had been, like it had never existed.

She forced herself to blink, to breathe, to make sense of what she was seeing.

But her body refused to move.

Because some part of her already knew.

He was gone.

The motel's flickering neon sign buzzed overhead.

The wind shifted.

And somewhere just beyond the reach of the light—

Something watched.

Dana could feel it.

Then, slowly, she stepped back inside and shut the door.

Click.

She turned the lock.

And for the first time since she had returned to Pine Hollow—

She was completely alone.

Chapter 6

Dana jolted awake, her breath shallow, her body rigid with unease. The motel room was too quiet. Not the kind of stillness that came with early morning drowsiness, but a hollow, unnatural silence that made her skin prickle. It took her a moment to place why that silence felt so wrong, why the emptiness pressed against her chest like a weight. Then it hit her—sharp, cold, undeniable. Ben.

She shot upright, heart hammering against her ribs as her gaze darted across the dim room. Ben had been here. She was sure of it. The last thing she remembered was the knocking at the door, the flickering lights, the way he had stepped outside. Then—nothing. A black void where memories should have been, a gap in her mind that made her stomach twist. She grabbed her phone off the nightstand, fingers trembling as she unlocked it, desperate for proof that he had existed outside of her own recollection.

Her call log was empty. No missed calls. No texts. No record of Ben at all. She scrolled through her messages, searching for something—anything—that would confirm he had been real. But every conversation, every exchange, every trace of him had been wiped clean. Panic coiled in her stomach as she dialed his number, clinging to the hope that this was some kind of mistake. The line rang once, then cut to an automated response.

"The number you have dialed is not in service." The voice was sterile, emotionless, absolute. Dana pulled the phone away and stared at the screen, disbelief curdling into dread. This wasn't right. This wasn't possible. He was real. He was real. But the world was already shifting, already pushing him out of existence, and she could feel it happening. Her breath came quick and shallow as she yanked her jacket from the chair, grabbed her keys, her bag—she had to go. She had to find him. Prove he was still here before he vanished entirely.

The drive to the station blurred past her, a rush of streetlights and empty roads she barely registered. She gripped the steering wheel so tightly her knuckles turned white, her mind racing with possibilities she refused to accept. Ben was real. He had to be. She would walk into the station, find him at his desk, hear his voice, see the exasperation in his eyes when he asked her why she looked like she'd seen a ghost. But as she pulled into the parking lot, dread settled deep in her bones. Ben's cruiser was gone. In its place sat a different squad car, one she didn't recognize.

Inside, the air smelled the same—coffee, old paper, something faintly metallic—but the familiarity ended there. Dana's pulse pounded in her ears as she approached the front desk, expecting to see a face she knew. Instead, the man behind the counter was a stranger. He was older, with graying hair and a uniform that looked like it had molded to his body over years of wear. He barely glanced up as she entered, his expression neutral, unbothered.

He looked up at her with a mild frown, his expression edged with polite curiosity. "Morning, ma'am. Something I can help you with?"

Dana paused, taking a sudden breath. Her mouth was dry, her thoughts scrambling to catch up. "I—I need to speak to Sheriff Reese."

The man's brow creased deeper. "Sheriff who?"

The air in her lungs turned to ice. "Ben Reese," she repeated, voice cracking at the edges. "He's the sheriff here."

The man's frown deepened, but there was no recognition in his eyes. "Miss, I've been sheriff here for twenty-two years."

The world tilted beneath her feet.

Twenty-two years. That meant Ben had never existed in this role. Never wore the badge. Never patrolled these streets. Never lived.

She gripped the edge of the counter, her nails digging into the wood. "No, that's—" The words cut off in her throat, strangled by the sick realization curling through her chest.

The truth settled like a weight against her ribs.

Because as far as the world was concerned… Ben had never existed.

Dana's pulse roared in her ears, drowning out everything but the sickening certainty creeping into her bones. She stared at the man—Sheriff Turner. The name felt wrong, like an ill-fitting puzzle piece forced into place. But there was no hesitation in his gaze, no flicker of uncertainty. He wasn't lying. He had been sheriff here for over two decades. To him, to everyone in this town, Ben had never worn the badge.

But that wasn't possible.

Dana's lips parted, her voice unsteady. "I—I must've misspoken. I meant Sheriff Ben Reese."

Turner's expression didn't change. If anything, the concern behind his eyes deepened. "Who?"

A cold fist tightened around Dana's ribs. She swallowed, forcing her voice to stay steady. "Ben Reese. He's been sheriff for the last five years."

Turner studied her for a beat, his expression shifting from mild concern to something closer to pity. "Miss," he said slowly, as if speaking to someone in distress, "I've been sheriff here for twenty-two years."

The words landed like a slap. A sharp, undeniable fracture in reality.

The floor felt unsteady beneath her, as if the very foundation of reality had shifted. Twenty-two years. That meant Ben had never been here—never taken over, never worn the uniform, never so much as stepped into this station in an official capacity. It wasn't just that he was missing. He had been erased.

Dana's grip on the counter tightened. "No, that's—" She cut herself off, inhaling sharply. She couldn't unravel here. She had to stay in control, had to keep her head. If she pressed too hard, if she let the panic show, Turner would see her as just another woman losing her grip.

She forced a weak, almost apologetic smile. "Sorry," she muttered. "It's been a long night."

Turner studied her for a moment, his gaze measuring but not unkind. He wasn't suspicious, not yet—just cautious, as if debating whether to press further. "You sure you're alright?"

No. Not even close.

But she nodded anyway. "Yeah. Just a mistake." The lie sat heavy on her tongue, but she forced it out, forced her expression to remain neutral. If she stayed any longer, if she let her questions spill out in a desperate frenzy, she'd be giving herself away.

Turner gave a slow, accepting nod. "Alright then."

Dana didn't linger. She turned sharply and walked out, her legs moving on instinct, her breath tight in her chest.

She stepped onto the street, the town unfolding before her in cruel, indifferent normalcy. The sun cast long morning shadows across the pavement, people strolled past, cars idled at intersections, life pressed forward—completely untouched. Everything looked exactly as it should, yet it was all wrong. Because Ben wasn't here.

Not just missing. Not just gone.

Erased.

A hole had been carved into the world where he used to be, and she was the only one who could feel its absence. The weight of it pressed against her ribs, sharp and unbearable. Ben had always been there—grumbling over paperwork, rolling his eyes at her, standing beside her in ways that had never needed words. And now, there was nothing.

She had never let herself think too much about what Ben meant to her. They weren't the kind of people who put things into words. But now, as she stood in a town that had rewritten itself to forget him, the truth lodged in her throat like a stone.

She had never felt so completely alone.

Dana forced herself to move, her steps slow, deliberate, mechanical. The town hummed around her, oblivious, as if nothing had changed. People chatted outside a café, a delivery truck idled near the curb, a man walked his dog with the ease of someone who had no idea the world had just rewritten itself.

She wanted to grab someone, shake them, scream until her throat was raw. Do you remember him? The question burned inside her, but she already knew the answer. No one did.

The only thing worse than losing Ben was knowing she was the only one left who remembered he had ever existed.

The only thing worse than losing Ben was being the only one left who knew he had ever existed.

And that was a loneliness she had never been prepared for.

Dana kept walking, though she had no destination in mind—only the desperate need to keep moving. The sheriff's office, the café, the bookstore on the corner—they all looked the same, untouched by the impossible shift that had gutted her world. She tried to find some thread of reality to cling to, something that hadn't changed, but everything felt distorted, hollow.

Her boots scuffed against the pavement, the familiar rhythm drowned beneath the casual hum of a town that didn't know it was broken. People moved around her, smiling, talking, existing in a world that had already erased someone she loved. Life continued, unbothered.

But her world had ruptured.

And nobody else could see it.

She wandered without thinking, her feet carrying her to the small park near the courthouse—the one with the too-green grass and the rickety wooden benches. The place had always felt slightly out of sync with the rest of Pine Hollow, too manicured, too staged, but today, it felt even more artificial. Like a backdrop for a life that no longer existed.

Dana sank onto a bench, her limbs heavy, her pulse still erratic. The rational part of her mind tried to reason with the impossible—maybe she was misremembering, maybe exhaustion had twisted her perception—but she knew better. This wasn't a trick of memory. The world itself had changed. Something had rewritten reality, stolen Ben from existence, scrubbed every trace of him from the town's collective history.

And there was nothing left of him but her memory.

Dana pressed her palms to her face and took a sharp, shuddering breath. Get a grip. But how was she supposed to? The world had folded in on itself, reality shifting like sand beneath her feet. The grief clawing at her chest wasn't just for Ben—it was for the truth, for her own sanity. If the world could do this to him, how long before it did the same to her?

Her stomach churned. It wasn't just that Ben was gone—it was the way the world had adjusted to his absence so effortlessly. There were no gaps, no loose ends, no sense that anything was missing at all. Pine Hollow had already moved on, not because they had forgotten him, but because he had never existed in the first place.

And maybe—if she wasn't careful—she'd start to believe it, too.

Dana sat hunched over, her fingers gripping the edge of the bench as if holding onto something tangible could anchor her to reality. The weight of it all—the loss, the void where Ben should have been—pressed against her chest, thick and suffocating. Every part of her screamed that she should be grieving, that she should be consumed by the ache of his absence. And yet—

It was gone.

Not eased. Not settled into something she could carry. Just… gone. The grief didn't linger, didn't fester the way loss always did. It had been pulled from her, as if something had reached into her chest and stripped the feeling away.

Like it had decided she was done mourning.

Dana took a deep breath. She sat up straighter, her spine rigid, alarm prickling at the edges of her awareness. Grief didn't vanish like that. It was supposed to stay, to root itself deep, to shape the days that followed. But this—this was unnatural. This was something else entirely.

A slow, creeping horror settled in her gut. This wasn't just about Ben anymore. Something in Pine Hollow was pulling strings, deciding what was remembered, what was erased, what was felt. It had taken Ben. It had rewritten history. And now, it was trying to dictate how much she was allowed to hurt.

And if she didn't stop it?

It would come for her next.

Dana pushed off the bench, her mind sharpening, pulse steadying into something colder, harder. Enough waiting. Enough second-guessing. Whatever was happening in Pine Hollow—whatever was stealing people from existence—it was real. And it had just tried to erase her grief along with Ben.

She needed proof. If memories could be rewritten, if entire lives could be erased, then somewhere, something had to show the seams. A crack in the perfect illusion. A record that hadn't been altered. She turned toward the street, her steps deliberate. The records office. That was where she would start.

Because if Ben had never existed—if history had been rewritten—then somewhere, there had to be evidence.

And Dana was going to find it.

The walk to the records office felt wrong. Not in any obvious way—nothing had changed, nothing looked out of place—but the sensation burrowed under Dana's skin. It was in the air, in the way the town felt stretched too thin, in the way her own presence felt observed.

People moved around her as they always had, but there was something off. A man crossed the street ahead of her—twice. A woman pushing a stroller glanced at Dana and whispered something under her breath. When Dana turned, she was gone. It was subtle, almost imperceptible, but it was there.

She wasn't imagining this.

The world was watching her now.

And it knew she was watching back.

The records office loomed ahead, its old brick and yellowed blinds just as unremarkable as ever. But when Dana reached for the door handle, a chill ran through her. A warning, deep in her bones.

She stepped inside.

The air was heavy, thick with something unseen. It wasn't just silence—it was the kind of stillness that came when a room expected you. The woman at the front desk—a stern-faced woman with thin glasses and graying hair—was already looking at her. She wasn't surprised to see Dana.

She had been waiting.

Dana swallowed hard, keeping her expression neutral as she stepped forward.

"I need to look through some old town records."

The woman's lips curved—not in a polite smile, not in curiosity.

In recognition.

"Of course you do," she murmured.

Dana forced her expression to stay neutral, stepping up to the desk. "I need to look through some old town records."

Marjorie's lips curved into a small smile. Not a polite one. Not quite right.

"Of course you do," she murmured.

Dana's stomach twisted. That wasn't a normal response. Not *What kind of records?* or *Do you have a case number?* Just... acceptance. As if this had all happened before. As if Marjorie Hale—her name tag gleamed under the dim fluorescent lights—had been expecting this exact request.

Dana didn't let her expression falter. She had learned long ago that when something wasn't right, you didn't flinch. You played along.

She gave a small, measured nod. "Yeah. Town census reports, law enforcement rosters, missing persons records."

Marjorie didn't ask why. She didn't hesitate or glance at a computer screen. She simply stood, smoothing the front of her blouse.

"Of course," she said smoothly. "Follow me."

Dana's boots scuffed against the floor as she trailed behind Marjorie down a narrow hallway. The office was quiet—too quiet. No other employees. No visitors. Just the two of them. The air smelled faintly of dust and something chemical, and the overhead lights buzzed, flickering once as they passed beneath them.

Marjorie led her into a back records room, lined wall to wall with file cabinets. She stopped beside one, resting a hand against the cool metal. Then she turned to Dana, her expression unchanged.

"These are the records you're looking for."

Dana hesitated. There was something too precise about the way she said it. Like she already knew what Dana would find. Or worse—what she wouldn't.

Still, she reached for the cabinet handle.

She wasn't leaving without answers.

The metal was cold beneath her fingertips, an unyielding barrier between her and the truth. She exhaled sharply and pulled the drawer open, her breath hitching as she took in the files inside. Names, dates, town records—each carefully arranged, each carrying the weight of lives documented and accounted for. But one file sat at the front, deliberately placed. A file that shouldn't exist.

Her name.

Dana Crowell.

Her stomach twisted. The paper looked aged, its edges slightly curled, the ink faded as if it had been sitting there for decades. But that didn't make sense. She had never lived in Pine Hollow as an adult, never been in any official records beyond school transcripts. And yet, here it was, waiting for her.

Behind her, Marjorie's voice was soft, almost amused. "Go on, dear. Open it."

Dana's fingers hesitated over the tab, her pulse thrumming in her ears. The file shouldn't be here. It couldn't be here. And yet, the weight of it in her hands was undeniable. Swallowing hard, she flipped it open.

The first page made her stomach drop.

A birth certificate—her own.

She scanned the document, her eyes darting over familiar details. The date was correct, the county seal stamped in the corner, everything seemingly in order. But the ink had faded unnaturally, the paper worn at the edges like it had existed far longer than it should have. Dana's throat tightened as an unsettling thought wormed its way into her mind.

This file wasn't just a record of her life.

It was a record of something older.

Like she had always been part of this town.

Longer than she should have been.

Dana flipped to the next page—and everything inside her went still.

A death certificate.

Her own name stared back at her, stark and final against the aged paper. The document was dated April 6, 2010. Her mind reeled. That date—she knew it. It wasn't just a random day; it was the night. The night Morgan disappeared. The night everything changed.

She gripped the page, half expecting it to disintegrate under her touch, half hoping it would prove itself a forgery. But it felt real. Too real. The weight of official documentation, the familiar bureaucratic formatting, the faint imprint of a county seal—it was all there.

No.

No, this wasn't possible. She was alive. She had left this town, built a life outside of it. And yet, the words printed in bold ink told a different story.

She inhaled sharply, forcing herself to turn to the next page, dreading what she might find.

And then, beneath the death certificate, a single handwritten phrase sent an icy shiver down her spine.

"Not yet."

Her breath caught in her throat.

"No," she whispered.

That wasn't possible. She was alive. She had left this town. She had a life outside of it.

She stared at the words, at the neat, printed letters declaring her dead.

And beneath it, in faint, handwritten script, was something worse.

Something that made her skin prickle with cold dread.

"Not yet."

Behind her, Marjorie exhaled softly, almost like a sigh.

"There's more, dear."

Dana didn't respond. She couldn't. Her body felt locked in place, fingers still curled around the paper that shouldn't exist. The weight of it in her hands was suffocating. It wasn't just the words, the impossible declaration of her death—it was the implication.

Someone had written this. Filed this. Declared it.

Not just a clerical error. Not some bureaucratic mistake.

It was intentional.

Dana turned the page, her breath coming short and shallow.

The next document sent a fresh wave of unease rolling through her stomach.

An address history.

But instead of listing the places she had actually lived—her college apartment, her temporary stay in the city—there was only one entry.

Pine Hollow, 1892 – Present.

Her pulse stuttered.

This had to be a mistake. Some clerical mix-up. A joke. Anything but what it suggested.

She flipped to the next page, hands shaking now.

A school record.

Except it wasn't hers.

The dates were wrong. The signatures at the bottom belonged to teachers who had died long before she was even born.

The more she turned, the more distorted her life became. Pieces of reality, rewritten and rearranged into something unrecognizable.

And then, at the very bottom of the stack—

A photograph.

Her fingers hesitated over the edges. The image was black and white, faded with age. She saw the trees first—dark silhouettes stretching toward the sky, framing a clearing at the edge of the woods.

Then the people.

A group of townsfolk, standing together in stiff postures, their expressions somber, their clothes belonging to an era long past.

And there, at the very edge of the photo, half-consumed by shadow—

Was her.

Dana.

The room tilted.

Dana's grip tightened around the photograph, her knuckles white. The girl in the picture—her—looked younger, maybe sixteen, the same age she had been when Morgan disappeared. But the photograph itself was far older than that. The paper had yellowed with time, the edges curling as if handled by countless others before her.

That wasn't possible.

She had never seen this photograph before. Had never been in this photograph before. And yet, there she was, standing at the edge of the clearing, captured in grainy black-and-white, as though she had belonged there all along.

Her heart pounded.

This wasn't just some clerical error or misplaced document. This was evidence of something deeper. Something that twisted reality, bending time and memory until the truth became unrecognizable.

Had she been here before?

Had she forgotten?

Dana's pulse roared in her ears. The death certificate, the altered records, this photograph—it all pointed to the same impossible conclusion.

Something had been waiting for her.

Something had always been waiting for her.

Her pulse hammered.

She forced herself to look at the photograph again, searching for some logical explanation, some flaw that would unravel this impossibility. But there was none. The girl in the image was unmistakably her—the same sharp angles of her face, the same wary eyes. She wasn't a relative, not some distant ancestor with an uncanny resemblance.

It was her.

Her stomach twisted.

The world around her felt too still, too quiet, as if it were waiting for her to piece it together. But the pieces refused to fit.

She turned the photo over.

A date had been written in delicate, looping cursive: April 6, 1892.

The breath left her lungs.

That date—she knew it. She had seen it before, just moments ago.

On her death certificate.

Dana swallowed hard, nausea coiling in her gut. This wasn't just a mistake. It wasn't just altered records or rewritten history.

It was a pattern.

Her fingers trembled as she set the photograph down, her mind racing through every impossible scenario. What if she had been here before? What if she had been part of something bigger than she could remember?

Behind her, Marjorie took a slow step forward, peering over her shoulder at the documents spread before them.

Her voice was soft, knowing.

"You were never supposed to leave, dear."

Dana stared at the photo, her breath shallow. It didn't make sense. It shouldn't make sense.

And yet, here it was. A picture of her in a time she had never lived, alongside people she had never met. A death certificate marking the end of her life, though she stood here, very much alive.

Her mind raced. If these records were real—if they had always been real—then what did that mean for her? Had she escaped something? Had she forgotten something? Or worse—had something made her forget?

The thought sent a cold shudder through her.

She ran her fingers over the photograph, tracing the blurred edges where her image faded into shadow. Someone had placed this here for her to find.

Someone wanted her to see it.

Dana inhaled sharply and turned to Marjorie, her pulse thudding against her ribs. "What the fuck is going on?"

Marjorie only smiled, tilting her head as if amused by the question. "Depends," she murmured. "Do you want the easy answer?"

Dana's jaw tightened. "I want the truth."

Marjorie sighed, almost as if she had expected that. She reached forward, tapping a single finger against the death certificate.

"The truth is slippery, dear," she said softly. "It doesn't always stay where you left it."

Dana's hands clenched into fists. "Try me."

Marjorie sighed, the kind of exhale that carried the weight of inevitability. Like she had been waiting for this moment for far longer than Dana could understand.

Then, without hesitation, she reached forward and turned the next page.

Dana's breath caught as her mother's handwriting stared back at her.

Scrawled across the aged paper, in familiar, hurried script, were four words.

"They don't want you to remember."

Her pulse pounded.

This wasn't just some strange clerical anomaly. This wasn't an error in documentation or a misplaced file. Her mother had left this message.

Dana traced the ink with her fingertips, as if touching the words would somehow make them clearer, more comprehensible. But there was nothing to interpret. The warning was simple. Direct.

Her mother knew.

She had always known.

A wave of nausea rolled through Dana's stomach. If her mother had understood what was happening, if she had left this message behind—then that meant this wasn't new. It wasn't a recent phenomenon.

It had been happening for a very, very long time.

Her throat tightened. She swallowed hard and lifted her gaze to Marjorie. "Who are they?"

Marjorie didn't answer right away. Instead, she glanced briefly at the dim fluorescent lights overhead as if checking for something unseen.

Then, softly, she said, "You already know."

The weight of Marjorie's words settled deep in her bones, pressing against something unspoken, something she didn't want to acknowledge.

But she did know.

She just didn't want to say it out loud.

A sound broke the silence.

Soft. Wrong.

A low hum, like an old electrical current vibrating through the air, barely perceptible at first. But then it deepened, growing louder, thrumming against her skin, rattling in her skull.

The fluorescent lights overhead flickered once. Twice.

Then, everything outside the records office went silent.

Dana turned toward the front windows, her pulse a tight, erratic rhythm in her chest. The town square lay beyond, bathed in the dull glow of morning light.

People stood motionless.

A man sat on a bench, mid-sip of his coffee, frozen in place. A woman pushing a stroller was caught mid-step, her head tilted just slightly, her eyes vacant. A child clutching their mother's hand had his mouth open, his expression trapped in the middle of a sentence he would never finish.

No one moved.

Not a breath. Not a twitch.

They just stood there.

And then—in perfect synchronization—they turned.

Not toward each other.

Not toward anything in particular.

They turned toward her.

The hum in the air deepened, vibrating in her skull.

Their heads moved in eerie, unnatural unison. Like puppets on strings.

And their eyes—

Were wrong.

Dana's entire body locked up.

She knew what she was seeing.

Knew what it meant.

They weren't them anymore.

A presence had settled over them—completely, fully.

Not like with Mr. Reece, where something had pushed through for a moment.

This was control.

This was a possession of an entire town.

And it was looking directly at her.

A hand settled on Dana's wrist.

Warm. Solid.

Miriam.

Dana whipped her head around. She hadn't heard the old woman enter, hadn't sensed her presence, but now she was here.

Her grip on Dana's wrist wasn't tight, but it was grounding.

"Don't move," Miriam murmured.

Her voice was calm. Steady.

The only voice in the world that still belonged to itself.

Dana's throat was dry. "What the hell is happening?"

Miriam's fingers tightened ever so slightly.

"They're listening now."

Dana didn't breathe.

Miriam's grip on her wrist was firm but steady, the only thing tethering her to reality as the world outside warped into something unnatural. The townspeople hadn't moved, hadn't spoken, hadn't so much as blinked.

But they were watching.

Dana's pulse roared in her ears. A heavy, oppressive silence settled over everything, thick and suffocating, as if the very air had become something aware.

Miriam's gaze remained fixed on the frozen figures outside. Her expression was unreadable, but Dana could sense it—the quiet calculation behind her stillness, the way she measured the situation with a kind of certainty Dana didn't have.

"They don't like you digging," Miriam said at last, voice barely above a whisper. "You should have known this would happen."

Dana forced herself to swallow, to push words past the knot tightening in her throat. "You knew."

Miriam didn't deny it.

Instead, she sighed—low, slow, almost tired. "We need to leave. Now."

Dana's legs felt sluggish, weighted by the gravity of what was happening. She hesitated, her mind still trying to process the impossible, but Miriam didn't give her time. She tugged lightly at Dana's wrist, just enough to break her paralysis.

As they moved toward the back exit, Dana risked one last glance through the front window.

The townspeople still hadn't moved.

But their presence pressed against her, heavy and expectant, as though they didn't need to follow.

As though they already knew she would come back.

Miriam shoved the door open, leading Dana into the cool night air. The instant they stepped outside, the hum cut off—abrupt and absolute, like a radio signal going dead.

Dana exhaled sharply, trying to shake the feeling that they had just escaped something far worse than a watching crowd.

Miriam pulled a set of keys from her coat pocket and strode toward an old, dented pickup truck parked in the alley.

"Get in."

Dana hesitated, still shaken. "Where are we going?"

Miriam opened the driver's side door and finally looked at her, her expression unreadable.

"Somewhere they can't reach you."

Dana swallowed hard but didn't argue. She climbed into the truck, slamming the door shut behind her.

As Miriam started the engine, Dana risked one last glance in the side mirror.

The town square remained eerily still. A few people had begun to move again, slow and mechanical, as if the world was winding itself back into motion.

But others—others hadn't moved at all.

They were still standing there.

Still watching.

Miriam pulled onto the road without another word, gripping the wheel tightly.

Dana forced herself to breathe, but the truth gnawed at her.

The Watchers hadn't tried to stop them.

Because they didn't need to.

Because they had time.

Miriam's voice was quiet, but final.

"They're patient."

They drove in silence for a long stretch, the empty backroads of Pine Hollow stretching long and dark before them. The town disappeared behind them, swallowed by the dense tree line, but Dana could still feel it. The weight of unseen eyes, the lingering presence of something that didn't need to chase them—because it already knew where they were going.

She clenched her hands into fists, pressing her nails into her palms. Miriam didn't speak. She kept her gaze fixed on the road ahead, her grip on the steering wheel tight but controlled, her silence speaking louder than words.

Dana's thoughts churned. The death certificate. The altered records. The photograph.

Had it all been waiting for her? Had she been meant to find it?

Or worse—had she been led to it?

Miriam finally turned off onto a narrow gravel road, the truck rattling slightly as it rolled over uneven terrain. The thick canopy of trees swallowed the sky, their skeletal branches twisting above them like reaching fingers.

The further they went, the heavier the air became.

Miriam's house came into view, tucked away at the edge of the trees, barely visible through the overgrowth. It looked untouched by time—worn but sturdy, the kind of place that had existed long before the town had reshaped itself around something unnatural.

Dana exhaled as the truck rolled to a stop.

They had made it.

But the unease in her chest only grew.

Miriam killed the engine and sat back with a sigh. She didn't move to get out, didn't look at Dana right away.

And then, finally, she spoke.

"I think it's time we talked about what's really happening to you."

Miriam's house was quiet.

Not the kind of quiet that came with solitude, but something deeper—intentional. The air inside felt heavy, thick with an unspoken presence that pressed against Dana's skin the moment she stepped over the threshold.

The space was cluttered but not messy. Shelves lined with old books, jars filled with things Dana didn't want to name, a fireplace stacked with wood that didn't look like it had been burned in years. In the far corner, a small table sat with two chairs—one slightly askew, as if someone had just stood up from it.

Everything in the house felt placed, as though none of it was there by accident.

Dana's gaze caught on a mirror against the far wall. It wasn't old, wasn't anything remarkable—just an ordinary, rectangular mirror in a dark wooden frame.

And yet—

She and Miriam stood in the doorway, but in the reflection, Dana swore she saw someone else. A faint shape. A figure just behind them.

She blinked.

It was gone.

A chill prickled at the back of her neck, but she forced herself to turn away.

"This place feels…" She hesitated, searching for the right word.

Miriam walked toward the kitchen, moving with slow deliberation. "Different?"

Dana exhaled. "Yeah. Different."

Miriam pulled two mismatched mugs from the cabinet, setting them on the table. She poured tea—not coffee, never coffee—and slid one toward Dana.

"You're remembering more, aren't you?"

Dana stared at the cup, fingers tightening around its edges. The liquid inside was still. Too still.

She swallowed. "I don't know what I'm remembering anymore."

Miriam took a slow sip of her own tea, watching Dana over the rim of her cup.

"Then we should start fixing that."

Dana wrapped her fingers around the mug, but didn't drink.

The warmth seeped into her palms, grounding her, but something about the stillness of the liquid inside unsettled her. It didn't steam, didn't ripple, as if frozen in time. She placed the cup back down, unease coiling tight in her chest.

Miriam was watching her. Not with suspicion, not with concern, but with something else—something deeper. A quiet knowing.

Dana should have been exhausted. Should have been overwhelmed, unraveling, something. But the fear, the grief, even the panic—it wasn't there.

Like it had been pulled from her.

She exhaled sharply, her voice steadier than she expected. "Start talking."

Miriam didn't flinch, didn't blink. She simply tilted her head slightly, like she had been waiting for Dana to say those words.

But instead of answering, she smiled—soft, almost amused.

"You've been asking the wrong questions, dear."

Dana's jaw clenched. "I'm not playing games with you."

Miriam set her cup down without a sound. Her expression remained unreadable, but the weight of her words lingered between them.

"You want to know what's happening," she said simply. "Why people are disappearing. Why the world is rewriting itself around you."

She leaned forward slightly—just enough for the words to settle deep.

"But what you should be asking, Dana, is why you were never taken, too."

The statement hit Dana like a punch to the chest. Her breath stalled, fingers loosening around the mug. Because Miriam was right. Morgan was taken. Erased. Ben was taken. Erased. But Dana? She had been at the very heart of it, standing at the edge of oblivion, and yet—she was still here.

She had always been here.

She should have disappeared that night in the woods.

And yet.

Something had let her stay.

Swallowing hard, she forced out the question that had been gnawing at her mind. "You remember Ben, don't you?"

Miriam nodded without hesitation.

Relief and dread curled in Dana's stomach in equal measure. "He's gone," she whispered. "Like he was never real. The sheriff's different. There's no trace of him. But you—" She shook her head, stepping closer. "You remember him."

Miriam's lips pressed into a thin line.

"I remember them all."

Dana's breath caught. Morgan. Ben. Miriam remembered everyone the town had forgotten.

A gust of wind rattled the window.

But it was wrong.

It didn't come from outside. Not from any draft.

It came from inside the house.

A slow, creeping current of air brushed the back of Dana's neck. She turned sharply, scanning the empty space behind her. Nothing. Only stillness.

Miriam watched her.

"Drink your tea, dear," she murmured. "You're going to need it."

Dana didn't touch the tea.

Instead, she stared at Miriam, her words settling like stones in her chest.

"I remember them all."

Morgan. Ben. Everyone else who had been taken—people she didn't even know about.

And the worst part?

Miriam had said it so plainly. Like it was just a fact of life. Like it had always been this way.

Dana exhaled slowly, forcing her voice to stay steady. "How?"

Miriam didn't blink. "How do I remember?"

Dana nodded.

Miriam leaned back in her chair, hands folded neatly in her lap.

"I'm not like you, dear."

Dana's stomach twisted. "What does that mean?"

Miriam's lips curled into something almost amused. "It means I've always seen the things most people choose to forget."

A prickle of unease crept up Dana's spine. "That's not an answer."

Miriam tilted her head slightly. "Isn't it?"

The air in the room grew heavier. Dana's pulse quickened. She could still feel the breath of wind that wasn't there. But Miriam—Miriam wasn't scared. She wasn't rattled.

She had been expecting all of this.

The town turning. The erasures. The Watchers.

And Dana.

Especially Dana.

Dana took a step forward, voice tight. "Then tell me why I wasn't taken."

Miriam exhaled, slow. Measured.

She studied Dana like she was looking at a puzzle with a missing piece.

Then, finally—

"I don't know."

Dana's fingers curled into fists. "Bullshit."

Miriam's gaze hardened.

"Do you think I would lie to you?" she asked, her voice low, even.

Dana's throat tightened.

Yes.

No.

She didn't know.

And that terrified her.

Another gust of unseen wind stirred through the house.

This time, the pressure in the air was stronger.

Like something was shifting.

Like something was closing in.

Miriam felt it, too.

Because for the first time since Dana had stepped into the house—her expression changed.

Her shoulders tensed.

Her jaw clenched.

Her fingers twitched—like she was about to reach for something.

And then—

The lights flickered.

Once.

Twice.

And then, from the dark corner of the room—

A whisper.

Soft. Crawling.

Dana.

The whisper curled through the air, crawling under Dana's skin.

Soft. Deliberate.

Like it wasn't just saying her name.

Like it was calling her.

Dana gasped.

She turned sharply toward the corner of the room—where there was nothing.

Nothing but shadow.

The kind of dark that wasn't just an absence of light.

The kind of dark that felt occupied.

Her pulse thundered.

Miriam stood slowly.

No fear. No rush.

Like she had been waiting for this, too.

The lights flickered again.

Once.

Twice.

And then—

The whisper came again.

Closer.

"Dana."

A chill sliced through Dana's spine. Her blood ran cold.

Because this time—

It was right behind her.

She spun on instinct, whipping around to face whatever was there.

But the space behind her was empty.

And yet, something was wrong.

The air had changed. It was thick and charged—alive in a way that defied reason. It pressed at the edges of her thoughts, not just present but probing and reaching.

Trying to push inside her mind.

Her breath caught. No. No. No.

Panic surged. She staggered back, pulse hammering, the unseen force closing in—

And then Miriam moved.

Fast.

Faster than Dana would have thought possible.

Her hand shot out, fingers closing around Dana's wrist in a firm, unyielding grip.

And the moment their skin touched—

The lights stabilized.

The whisper stopped.

The presence recoiled.

Dana sucked in a sharp breath, the crushing weight lifting just enough for her to breathe again.

Miriam exhaled through her nose, slow and steady, her composure unshaken.

Then, without hesitation—so calm it made Dana's stomach twist—

She turned toward the corner of the room.

And she said, flat, unafraid:

"Not yet."

The shadows deepened.

The air thinned.

And just like that—

The presence was gone.

Dana yanked her wrist free, chest rising and falling in sharp bursts.

Her body was shaking.

Not just from fear—but from something deeper.

Something that had almost gotten inside.

She turned to Miriam, demanding. "What the hell was that?"

Miriam just sighed.

And then, with that same measured calm, she sat back down.

"You're asking the right questions now."

Dana's skin still crawled.

The whisper was gone, but it left something behind. A presence, an impression—a weight she couldn't shake. Something had just tried to get into her.

And Miriam had stopped it.

Dana's breath came too fast, too shallow. She pressed her palms against the table, grounding herself. Then, through gritted teeth—"What the hell was that?"

Miriam took her time answering. She reached for her tea again, lifting the cup with steady fingers. Unshaken. Unmoved. Like this was just another day. Like Dana hadn't just been whispered to by something that wasn't there. She sipped slowly, set the cup down. Then she finally looked at Dana.

"Something that almost got through."

Dana's stomach turned. She had felt it. That split second where something had tried to push into her mind, into her thoughts. And that whisper—it had known her name. Not like a ghost, not like some echo from the past. It had been aware. It had been trying to reach her.

Dana's hands clenched. "What did you do?"

Miriam studied her, fingers laced over her knee.

"I reminded it that you're not ready."

Dana's pulse kicked. "Ready for what?"

Miriam's lips curved just slightly. "For them to take you back."

Silence.

Heavy. Thick.

Dana's mouth felt dry. Something inside her twisted, recoiled.

Take her back. Not take her. Take her BACK.

Like she had already been theirs once before.

She took a step back, her breath coming uneven now.

Miriam just watched. Measured. Unshaken.

Dana swallowed past the lump in her throat. "You knew."

Miriam didn't deny it. "I suspected."

Dana's fingers curled against the table edge. "Suspected what?"

Miriam sighed. "That you were touched by them before."

Dana's pulse pounded. The world around her felt too small. Too tight. Because that word—touched. It felt right.

Not in a comforting way. In a way that made her stomach turn. Like a puzzle piece that had finally clicked into place. Like an answer she had been trying to avoid.

Dana's voice shook. "What do they want?"

Miriam exhaled through her nose. And when she spoke, her voice was quiet. Almost gentle. "You already know."

Miriam reached out. Gently. Deliberately. Her fingers were warm as they wrapped around Dana's hand, enclosing it between both of hers.

Not forceful. Not demanding.

Just holding.

And then, she lifted Dana's hand close to her mouth. And whispered—

"You already know."

The room vanished.

Not literally.

Not physically.

But Dana wasn't in it anymore.

Because everything crashed back into her.

The woods stretched before her. The towering pines stood too tall, too still, their presence pressing in like silent sentinels. The air was thick—dense with something unseen, something watching.

Morgan ran ahead, her laughter light, effortless—until it wasn't. The flash of her jacket disappeared between the trees, her joy warping into something else. A scream. Sharp. Cut short.

Dana saw herself, frozen at the threshold.

And she remembered.

She hadn't just witnessed Morgan vanish. She had been there, too. The woods had taken her.

She had felt it—the shift, the pull, the unnatural warping of reality around her. She had crossed over. Just for a moment.

And for that moment, however long it lasted—She hadn't been here anymore. She had been somewhere else.

Then, without reason or explanation—She had been sent back.

Dana gasped, stumbling backward. The room around her swayed, her breath coming fast and ragged as reality fought to steady itself.

She knew.

She knew what had happened.

She knew what was taking people.

She knew why no one remembered.

She knew what it meant to be taken back.

But there was still one thing missing.

She turned to Miriam, her heart hammering, voice hoarse. "What are you?"

Silence.

Miriam held her gaze for just a moment.

Then—

She was gone.

Not like someone leaving the room. Not like stepping into the next space. One second, she was there.

The next—

Nothing.

No sound. No movement. No trace of her at all. Just empty space where she had been sitting.

Dana's stomach twisted.

This wasn't just disappearing. This was something else. Something bigger. Older.

She exhaled sharply, rubbing a hand down her face.

Miriam hadn't just been some old woman who knew too much.

She was something else. Something powerful.

Dana turned in a slow circle, scanning the silent, empty house.

Miriam was gone.

And yet—Dana could still feel her. The air carried her presence, as if the house itself remembered. As if she was still watching.

And the worst part? Dana understood why she left.

Dana now knew there were others. Within the Watchers. Older. Stronger. Much more powerful than the whispers that torment her.

And they wouldn't tolerate interference.

She inhaled, steadying herself.

She was alone. But she wasn't lost. Because now, she knew.

She knew what had to be done.

She knew how to stop this.

And for the first time since returning to Pine Hollow—

She wasn't afraid anymore.

Chapter 7

Dana sat in the silence, her pulse finally slowing. The weight of everything that had happened pressed into her chest, grounding her in the moment. Miriam was gone—not dead, not erased, just… elsewhere. That realization settled in her mind like a puzzle piece clicking into place. Miriam wasn't like the others. She wasn't like Dana. And now, for the first time, Dana understood why.

Dana exhaled slowly, pressing her palms against the wooden table. Her mind was full, but not in the frantic, overwhelming way she had grown accustomed to. This wasn't chaos. This was something else—something final. The scattered fragments of understanding had settled, aligning into a truth she could no longer ignore. It had always been there, just out of reach. But now, at last, she understood.

This had never been just about missing persons. It wasn't just a town with a dark past. It was the cycle—it had always been the cycle. People had disappeared from Pine Hollow for generations, long before Dana was born, long before anyone living could recall. It had been happening for as long as the town had existed. And yet, no one ever remembered. That was the point.

Pine Hollow was more than just a town. It was a threshold—a place where reality frayed at the edges, where something ancient reached through. The Watchers, the ones who erased, the ones who decided, had shaped this place into something unnatural.

Dana had been claimed once. She had been taken, just like the others. But unlike them, she came back. She wasn't supposed to. She should have been forgotten, erased, absorbed into whatever lay beyond that threshold. And yet, she was here.

Something had gone wrong.

The pieces of the past tumbled through her mind, their edges sharp, refusing to fit neatly together. Morgan had been taken. Erased. Ben had been taken. Erased. But Dana? She had been let go. Or worse—rejected. A flaw in the pattern. A mistake in the cycle.

The Watchers hadn't stopped her before. They had let her go, unchallenged, unwatched. And now she understood why. They had always known she would return. She had to. The cycle wouldn't let her go.

Her fingers curled into fists.

Her mother had known. That was why she had left the book, the warnings, the messages hidden in the corners of Dana's past. That was why Miriam had intervened, why the town itself had started to shift, reacting to Dana's presence.

They had allowed her to walk away once. But they wouldn't make that mistake again.

Dana exhaled slowly and pushed herself up from the chair. This time, she felt steady. Grounded. Because now, she understood. She wouldn't be another piece in their pattern. She wouldn't let this continue. She was going to break the cycle.

No matter what it took.

Dana paced, her thoughts shifting and reforming, pieces of a larger truth still unsettled in her mind. But one question refused to fade.

Miriam.

She hadn't been erased. She hadn't been rewritten. The Watchers had power over this town, over its people, yet Miriam had stood outside of that power. She had defied them. And they had let her.

That wasn't normal. That wasn't human.

Dana exhaled sharply and dropped back into the chair, pressing a hand over her face. She had spent so much time chasing the missing—those taken, those erased, those who had vanished without a trace. But she had never stopped to consider something just as important.

Who had been left behind?

Miriam had remained. Through every cycle, every disappearance, every rewriting of history—she had always been here. The town had shifted, memories had been stolen, people had vanished into nothing. But not Miriam.

Because she was never meant to be erased.

So what did that make her?

A survivor? No. That word wasn't right. This wasn't luck, and it wasn't an accident. Miriam hadn't avoided the Watchers' influence by chance. She had existed outside of it.

Dana thought about the way Miriam spoke—the quiet certainty, the way she observed the town, as if none of it surprised her. As if she had seen this happen before. Not once. Not twice. Many times.

And when she left—it wasn't like Ben. It wasn't like Morgan. She hadn't been erased.

She had simply gone.

Like she had somewhere else to be.

Dana's gaze drifted to the cold tea on the table, to the stillness of the house—a house that, somehow, had never truly felt like it belonged to Miriam at all.

"You were never supposed to leave, dear."

Was that a warning? Or regret?

Miriam had said she would be watching. Not helping. Not guiding. Watching.

But why?

Because she had already done what she could. And now, Dana had to do the rest alone.

The chair scraped softly against the wooden floor as Dana stood. Miriam had given her answers—more than she ever expected. But was it all of them?

Had Miriam really told her everything? Or, like everyone else in this town, had she only given Dana what she was meant to hear?

A fresh wave of unease curled through her.

Dana wasn't leaving until she was sure.

Dana turned back toward the house, scanning the space with fresh eyes.

Miriam was gone, but this place—**this house that felt older than it should, heavier than it should**—remained. And if Miriam had left behind any truths she hadn't spoken aloud, maybe, just maybe, they were hidden somewhere within these walls.

She started in the living room.

The bookshelves were packed tightly with mismatched spines, some cracked with age, others curling at the edges. As Dana traced her fingers along them, a thin layer of dust clung to her skin. Some of these books were old—but not just old.

They were preserved.

Not merely collected, not merely stored. Guarded.

Her fingers skimmed the spines, moving instinctively, until—she stopped.

One felt different.

The leather was smooth. Too smooth. Unlike the others, this one hadn't cracked with time or gathered dust. It didn't belong.

Dana tugged at it.

It didn't budge.

Her pulse kicked up. She gripped the spine tighter, bracing herself, and pulled again—harder.

A quiet click echoed through the stillness.

The shelf shifted.

Not much. Just enough.

And Dana knew—something was hidden here.

The bookshelf gave under Dana's grip—just barely. A fraction of an inch, a slight shift in weight. But it was enough.

Something was behind it.

Her breath caught. Miriam had secrets. And now, one of them was about to belong to Dana.

She pressed against the edge, testing its weight. The shelf resisted at first, but then, slowly—deliberately—it moved. A narrow gap appeared behind the books, the space dark and undisturbed.

Dana leaned in, heart pounding.

A compartment. Small. Hidden. Waiting.

Inside, there was only one thing.

A box. Small, wooden, hand-carved.

Dana reached for the box, fingers brushing over its smooth, timeworn surface. It was simple, unadorned—but heavy in a way that had nothing to do with weight.

It wasn't locked.

She flipped the lid open.

And froze.

Inside, wrapped in thin, yellowed fabric, was a single photograph.

Not old like the others. Not a relic of the past.

This was new.

Crisp. Modern. Recent.

Dana's fingers trembled as she lifted it. And the moment her eyes focused, a chill coiled through her veins.

It was a photo of her.

She stood in the middle of the Pine Hollow woods, the trees stretching high above, the shadows twisting unnaturally behind her. The composition was off—wrong in a way she couldn't name.

But that wasn't the worst part.

The worst part—the thing that made her stomach knot, her breath falter—was the simple, impossible truth.

She had never taken this photo.

She had never stood in that spot.

She had never been there.

But someone had.

And they had been watching her.

Dana took a sudden breath.

She lifted the photo higher, scanning every inch under the dim light. The woods, her own face, the stretch of trees behind her—so familiar yet distant.

And then—the shadow.

A figure loomed in the background, just behind her, deep within the trees. Too far to make out details, but close enough to be undeniable.

Close enough to be watching.

A chill prickled down her spine.

This wasn't just a photograph. It was proof.

Proof that someone—or something—had been following her. Documenting her. There, in the woods, at a time she couldn't recall.

She tried to remember—tried to place the moment, the setting, the angle—but her mind came up blank.

It was as if the image had been plucked from a reality that wasn't hers.

Or worse—a reality she had already forgotten.

Her fingers trembled as she turned the photograph over. A single line of handwriting was scrawled across the back.

Familiar. Unmistakable.

Her mother's.

"You are not alone."

Dana's grip on the photograph tightened.

The figure. The shadowed presence.

It was the same feeling she'd had at the funeral—the same eerie, unshakable certainty that something had been there, just beyond the veil of her perception. She hadn't imagined it then. She wasn't imagining it now.

This was real.

And whoever—**or whatever**—this was, they weren't done watching her.

She forced herself to look at the writing again.

"You are not alone."

Her mother had known.

She had tried to warn her.

But was this meant as comfort?

Or a threat?

Dana swallowed hard, her pulse unsteady.

She had spent so much time chasing the missing—Morgan, Ben, all the countless others erased from Pine Hollow's past. But now, for the first time, she wasn't sure if she should be looking for them.

Or watching her own shadow.

Because someone was already looking for her.

And this time, they weren't hiding.

Dana kept her head low as she walked, sticking to the back roads, the tree-lined paths—the spaces where the town couldn't see her all at once.

She hadn't seen another soul since leaving Miriam's.

That was a good thing.

Because the Watchers weren't chasing her.

They were waiting.

She could feel it—not as eyes on her back, not as footsteps in the distance, but as presence. A weight pressing into the edges of her mind, like a whisper that never quite reached her ears.

They were patient. Watching. Waiting.

Which meant she had to move first.

She had to go back—one last time.

The Crowell house stood exactly as she had left it. Silent. Unmoved by time.

She hesitated at the threshold, an unsettling thought curling through her mind. Had the house changed? Would the things she had uncovered still be there? Or had the town rewritten them, erased them, made them into something else?

Only one way to find out.

Dana pushed open the door. Unlocked. Just as she had left it.

Inside, the air was still.

The dust had settled undisturbed, the furniture sat untouched. Everything was exactly as she had left it.

And yet, something was different.

Not in the way the town changed, not in the way the Watchers erased things.

This was something else.

Like the house knew she was coming.

Like it had been waiting.

She moved through the house carefully, deliberately.

Her mother had left her messages—one after another. Warnings. Clues. Pieces of a truth she had only just begun to understand.

Had she missed something?

The air inside felt thick, expectant. The house was silent, but it wasn't empty.

Dana's fingers trailed over the bookshelves, the furniture—the spaces her mother had spent the most time. If there was something left behind, something hidden, she would find it.

Then—she froze.

A presence. A shift in the air, subtle but undeniable.

Someone was outside.

Dana's head snapped toward the window.

A figure stood just beyond the tree line.

Not motionless like the others she had seen before. Not empty.

This one was waiting.

And then—he moved.

Dana felt him before she truly saw him. A presence unlike the Watchers—hesitant, uncertain.

She took a slow step forward, fingers twitching at her sides. Not fear. Not yet.

She turned.

A man stood at the edge of the woods.

Not frozen. Not blank-faced and hollow-eyed like the controlled townspeople.

He was breathing.

Dark-haired, mid-thirties, his stance too tense for someone simply lost. His posture wasn't rigid, wasn't unnatural.

He was different.

Because he wasn't watching her.

He was waiting.

Dana's fingers itched toward her pocket, even though she had nothing to reach for.

Her voice was sharp. "Who are you?"

The man's expression tightened. He shifted slightly, his weight shifting back, like the question unsettled him.

Then—a beat. A hesitation. And he spoke.

"I… don't know."

The words struck something deep inside her. Not because they were strange. But because they felt true.

Dana took a slow step forward, scanning his face, his stance, the uncertainty bleeding into his expression.

He wasn't playing games. He didn't know. His own name. His own reason for being here. And yet, here he was.

Dana studied him, the slow burn of recognition in his eyes. Not clear, not sharp, but there.

Like he knew her. Like something inside him was trying to remember her. The same way something inside her knew she should trust him.

Not because she had reason to. But because Miriam had led him here. She could feel it.

Just like she had felt the pull back to Pine Hollow. Just like she had felt the moment Ben disappeared.

He was supposed to be here.

His gaze flicked toward the house, his brow furrowing—not in confusion, but frustration. Like it meant something to him. Like he had seen it before.

"I…" He exhaled, pressing his fingers against his temple. "I don't know why, but I had to come here."

Dana's stomach tightened.

Miriam.

This was her doing. She had sent him. But why?

And more importantly—Who was he?

Dana didn't question it. Not the way she should have. Not the way she normally would. She just knew.

She nodded toward the door. "Come inside."

The man hesitated. His voice was quiet. "You trust me?"

Dana held his gaze. "Yeah. I do."

And somehow, that was enough. The moment Dana closed the door behind them, she felt it.

The shift.

Like a crack in the foundation of something far bigger than she understood. Something had been disturbed. Something that was meant to remain untouched. And the Watchers were not going to let it go unnoticed.

He stepped inside, his movements slow, measured. His eyes scanned the room like it was familiar and foreign at the same time. Like he had been here before, but couldn't remember when.

Dana watched him carefully. "You sure you don't know why you're here?"

He exhaled, his jaw tightening. "…I thought I didn't."

He dragged a hand through his hair, frustration flickering in his expression.

"But now—" He stopped, pressing his fingers to his temple. "I think I do."

Dana's pulse picked up.

He was remembering. And that meant something was slipping. Something the Watchers hadn't accounted for.

She stepped closer, keeping her voice steady. "What do you remember?"

He inhaled deeply, his brow furrowing. Then—he lifted his gaze to hers. And for the first time since she'd met him, his expression sharpened.

"I was taken."

Dana's stomach tightened. She had known it. Felt it. But hearing him say it—confirm it—made it real.

He blinked, his breathing shallow.

"I remember running. Not from something. Toward something."

His hands curled into fists. "And then…" His voice dropped. "Nothing."

His eyes flickered with something dark. Unsteady.

"But I wasn't alone."

A chill ran down Dana's spine.

She swallowed hard. "Who was with you?"

His hands twitched. Then, slowly, painfully—he shook his head.

"I don't know," he muttered, voice hoarse. "But I think…"

He stopped.

Pressed his fingers harder into his temple, like something was clawing its way back. Then—his body jerked forward, hands slamming onto the table.

The air in the room crackled. Dana took a step back as the lights dimmed. The walls felt too close. The weight in the room thickened.

His hands trembled against the wood.

Like something was fighting to pull him back. Like he was being claimed again.

His eyes snapped up to hers—wide, wild, desperate.

"Dana."

The shadows stretched. The floorboards creaked.

And outside, in the distance—Something knocked.

Soft.

Measured.

Deliberate.

Like it knew. Like it was waiting.

Because he had broken free. And now, they wanted him back.

His breathing steadied, but his fingers still twitched against the tabletop.

The room felt wrong. Not like before, when the Watchers had pressed in, when the lights had dimmed and the world itself had seemed to shift. This was subtler. More insidious. Like something in the air had changed, stretching around them like a presence neither of them could see.

Dana forced herself to push forward.

"You said you were taken," she murmured. "Do you remember when?"

He hesitated. "I—" He stopped.

Brows furrowing. Fingers flexing. A flicker of something unsteady crossed his face. Then—confusion.

"I don't… I don't know."

A chill ran down Dana's spine.

The hesitation wasn't right. It wasn't just forgetting. It was struggling. Like something inside him was fighting against itself.

She studied him carefully. "Think. Try to remember your name."

He closed his eyes as if concentrating as hard as he ever has.

"Caleb… Caleb Vance"

Dana responds "What year was it before you came here?"

Caleb frowned. "I—" His mouth opened, then closed. His jaw clenched, his fingers tightening into a slow fist.

Then, almost uncertainly:

"…1979?"

The words landed like a physical blow.

Dana's pulse spiked, her breath catching.

Caleb must have seen the shift in her expression because he straightened, tension bristling across his shoulders.

"What?" he asked, sharper now. "What's wrong?"

Dana swallowed hard.

"Caleb…" She exhaled, forcing herself to stay calm. "That was over forty years ago."

The air went still. Not normal still. Not like a room settling into silence. Still like a pause between heartbeats.

Caleb stared at her, his expression unreadable. Then he let out a short, breathless laugh.

"You're messing with me."

Dana shook her head. "No."

Caleb's lips parted slightly, something cracking beneath his exterior.

"That's… not possible."

Dana pushed forward. "Caleb. What do you remember after that?"

He began breathing irregularly. His fingers twitched again. And for the first time since they had met, his hands shook.

"…Nothing," he whispered.

The house creaked. Not loudly. Just enough. Just one step too many for an empty house.

Caleb's gaze flicked up toward the ceiling, and for a moment, neither of them breathed.

Then—outside, the trees shifted. Not with the wind. With something else. Something that had been waiting.

Watching.

And now, it knew.

Caleb's breath shuddered.

The weight of it—the truth, the time lost—settled over him like something suffocating.

He shook his head, disbelief tightening in his jaw.

"No," he muttered. "No, that doesn't make sense."

Dana watched him closely. "But it's true."

Caleb exhaled, running a hand over his face. "I don't feel forty years older."

"You're not."

Caleb's fingers froze. His breath caught.

Dana swallowed hard. "Caleb… look at yourself. You should be in your seventies."

Silence.

Thick, suffocating, unreal.

Caleb clenched his jaw, his fingers digging into his arms.

"But I remember that year," he whispered. "I remember it."

His voice was tight now, raw with something unspoken.

"I remember my house. I remember my truck. I remember—"

He cut himself off. Frowning. Like the thoughts in his head weren't aligning right. Like he was reaching for something that wasn't there anymore.

"…I remember a bar."

Dana's stomach tightened.

Caleb blinked, his breath shallow. He wasn't seeing her anymore. He was remembering.

"There was a bar," he murmured. "Just outside of town. Small. Wood panels. Always smelled like beer and cigarettes."

His fingers twitched again.

"There was a girl," he added, his voice distant. "She used to sit at the counter. Red hair. Always chewing gum. She—"

His words cut off suddenly. His entire body tensed. His expression twisted, pained. Like something had just yanked him back. Like something had just reached into his skull and torn it away.

Dana's pulse hammered.

"Caleb." She reached for him, but he flinched.

His hands gripped his head, hard.

"I—" He sucked in a breath, ragged and uneven. "I can't see her face."

His fingers pressed harder into his scalp, his body locking up.

"I just—I just had it." His voice cracked, panic creeping in. "I just—"

Then, suddenly—The lights flickered.

Dana stilled.

Caleb did too.

The bulbs overhead buzzed, the filaments inside whining under some unseen pressure. A deep, sharp creak echoed through the house. Like something settling. Like something pushing in.

Caleb gasped.

Dana could feel it now.

The Watchers knew. They had been waiting for this. And now, they were trying to take it back.

Caleb slammed his fist onto the table.

The moment his knuckles hit the wood, the lights stabilized. The house went still. But Dana knew better. That wasn't the end of it. It was just the beginning.

She met Caleb's gaze.

His eyes were wild now, sharp with realization.

"I wasn't supposed to remember," he whispered.

And Dana's stomach sank.

Because he was right. And now, they were both in deeper than before.

Caleb's hands were still shaking. His breath uneven.

Dana could see it—the strain, the struggle.

He wasn't just remembering. He was fighting to keep it.

And something was fighting back.

A noise thudded outside. Not a knock. Not footsteps. Something heavier.

Dana's head snapped toward the window.

Caleb's fingers curled against the table. "What was that?"

Dana didn't answer. Because she already knew. They weren't alone anymore.

The air in the room shifted. Not colder. Not hotter.

Thicker.

Like something unseen had stepped inside with them.

Caleb inhaled sharply, eyes darting toward the window. "Dana—"

Then—The front door creaked. Slow. Measured.

A pressure settled over the house. Something was here. And it was letting them know.

Dana grabbed Caleb's wrist.

His pulse was pounding beneath her fingertips.

She didn't look at him.

She just whispered—"Don't move."

The house groaned.

Caleb's body stiffened. His breath was ragged now, unsteady. But he didn't speak. He didn't dare.

Because outside—The wind wasn't blowing. But the trees were moving.

A shadow passed across the window.

No footsteps.

No sound.

Just movement.

Caleb's fingers tensed against hers.

The moment stretched. Too long. Too wrong. Then—A whisper. Faint. Right behind them.

"He doesn't belong."

Dana took a sharp breath.

Caleb jerked violently, pushing back from the table, his chair scraping against the floor.

He heard it too. The voice was real. But there was no one else in the house.

Caleb's chest rose and fell in sharp, heavy breaths.

Dana forced herself to stay calm. To think.

They had crossed a line. This wasn't just about watching anymore. The Watchers wanted Caleb back. And now, they were done waiting.

The lights flickered again.

Then—The front door knob turned. The doorknob twisted. Slow. Deliberate.

A sound so small—but it sent ice through Dana's veins. Her grip on Caleb tightened.

They couldn't stay. Not now. Not yet. They didn't know enough.

And whatever was on the other side of that door…

It did.

Dana moved first. Her body acted before her mind could catch up. Her fingers dug into Caleb's wrist, yanking him toward the back door.

Caleb hesitated for half a second—too long.

"Dana—"

The door creaked open.

Dana didn't look back. She couldn't.

"Move."

Caleb snapped into motion. He followed as she tore through the kitchen, feet slamming against the floor.

She hit the back door hard, nearly tearing it off its rusted hinges.

Outside, the air was too thick. Too wrong.

But at least out here—they could run. They didn't stop. Not to breathe. Not to think. The ground blurred beneath them, the trees closing in.

Dana's mind spun. Where? Where could they go? Nowhere in town was safe. Not anymore. They had to get out.

At least until they understood what they were really up against.

Caleb barely kept pace beside her. His breath was ragged, his strides long but unsteady.

Dana could feel it. The weight of the memories clawing at him. The time he shouldn't have lost. The thing they had tried to take back. And now, the Watchers were coming for him again.

Something moved behind them. Not footsteps. Not running.

Just… a shift.

Like the trees themselves were closing in.

Caleb glanced back.

Dana yanked him forward.

"Don't. Look. Back."

Dana didn't slow down. Not when her lungs burned. Not when her legs screamed.

They had to get out. Because if she was right—if the Watchers' power was tied to Pine Hollow itself—Then maybe, just maybe, they could outrun it.

Caleb's breathing was ragged beside her.

"Dana—" He coughed, barely keeping up. "Where the hell—"

"Away," she panted. "We need to get away."

She risked a glance back. Still no figures. No shapes in the trees. But that didn't mean they weren't there.

Watching.

Waiting.

Caleb stumbled. Dana caught his arm, yanking him forward. "Keep moving."

He didn't fight her. Even though his expression was tight with pain. Even though something behind his eyes was still breaking apart, trying to come back.

Dana clenched her jaw.

If they could just get outside the town limits... Maybe whatever was trying to take Caleb back wouldn't be able to reach him.

The trees thinned ahead.

Dana's chest tightened with hope.

The main road. If they could just—

CRACK.

The sound split the air like a gunshot.

Caleb jerked to a stop, eyes wide.

Dana froze.

The sound hadn't come from behind them. It had come from ahead. The road should have been there. She could see the faint gleam of asphalt through the trees. But something was wrong.

The air ahead shimmered. Shifted. Not a wall. Not a visible barrier. Something worse. The space in front of them wasn't right.

Dana's stomach dropped.

"Shit," she whispered.

Caleb turned to her, face pale.

"What?"

Dana swallowed hard.

"They know what we're trying to do."

The air wasn't air anymore. Not in the way it should have been. It shimmered in front of them, not a wall, not an object, but something else. Something that shouldn't exist.

Dana's breath shallowed.

They were trapping them in.

Caleb took a slow step forward, brow furrowing.

"What the hell is that?"

Dana grabbed his arm before he could get too close.

"I don't know," she admitted, heart hammering. "But I don't think we should touch it."

Caleb stared at it. At the way the space in front of them shifted, warped.

It wasn't blocking them, not exactly. But it was wrong. Like the world beyond it wasn't real anymore.

Caleb paused his breathing. His fingers twitched at his sides. Something about it was stirring something deep inside him. And then—his hands curled into fists.

"I've seen this before," he murmured.

Dana's eyes snapped to him.

His expression had gone tight. Pale.

Like a memory had just ripped through him.

Dana grabbed his wrist.

"Caleb," she said, voice steady but firm. "What do you remember?"

Caleb shook his head. Not in denial—in fear.

"It was like this," he whispered, eyes flickering with something raw.

His breathing turned uneven. His fingers twitched against his palms.

Dana could feel it—something clawing its way back to him.

"I was…" His voice was strained.

Then, his whole body tensed. His lips parted slightly, like something had just clicked into place.

And then—

"I didn't run."

Dana blinked. "What?"

His gaze was locked onto the shifting space ahead of them, but he wasn't seeing it anymore.

"I wasn't running from something," he muttered.

His voice was distant like he was standing in two places at once.

"I was running to something."

Dana's stomach tightened.

"Caleb, to what?" she pushed.

Caleb shook his head. A flicker of pain flashed across his face, sharp and raw.

"I don't know," he admitted, his voice almost a rasp. "I just—"

His eyes darkened. Like something had just clicked. Like something inside him had been stolen back.

And then—the ground beneath them rumbled.

Dana's breath caught.

Caleb stumbled back, eyes wide.

And just beyond the shifting air in front of them—

Something moved.

Not a person.

Not a shadow.

Something else.

Something waiting.

Something watching.

And Dana realized too late—They weren't escaping. They were being herded. Dana's stomach twisted. The realization settled in her bones like ice. They weren't being blocked. They were being funneled.

She could feel it now—the way the space around them had subtly shifted, guiding them, narrowing their options until this was the only place left to run.

And something was waiting.

Caleb took a slow step back, his breath uneven.

His hands curled into fists at his sides.

Dana could see it—the fight or flight reaction kicking in, his body remembering things his mind still couldn't grasp.

"We can't go that way," he muttered.

Dana barely breathed. "No."

Caleb's jaw tightened.

"So where the hell do we go?"

Something moved in the shifting air ahead. Not a shape. Not a shadow. Just a wrongness. Like a distortion in reality itself.

Dana took a sharp breath.

"We go back," she said.

Caleb snapped his gaze to her. "Back?"

Dana's pulse was hammering.

"We can't go forward. We need another way. Back through the trees, find a road that isn't blocked—"

Her voice cut off.

Because behind Caleb, through the gaps in the trees—Something was standing on the road.

Dana froze.

Caleb must have seen her expression shift because he whipped around. His breath shuddered out of him.

A figure.

Still. Too still. Standing just beyond the treeline. Waiting. The shadows stretched. The figure didn't move. Didn't blink.

Just watched.

Like it knew they had no way out.

Dana's fingers twitched toward Caleb's wrist.

"We need to move," she murmured.

Caleb didn't answer.

Because the moment she spoke—The figure tilted its head. And took a step forward.

Dana yanked Caleb back.

"Run."

He didn't argue. Didn't hesitate. Because the moment she said it—the figure moved. Not slow. Not measured. Fast.

Too fast.

And the last thing Dana saw before she turned—

Were its eyes.

And they were already watching them too closely. Dana didn't look back. She couldn't.

Caleb was already running beside her, his breath sharp and ragged, his boots kicking up dirt and leaves.

The trees blurred past them. The wind didn't move. The forest was too still. And yet—

Something was moving with them.

Dana felt it before she heard it. A shift in the air. A distortion in space itself. Then—a sound. Not footsteps. Not breathing. Something worse.

A low, hollow scrape that crawled down her spine like a whisper with no voice.

"Faster," she hissed, her grip tightening on Caleb's wrist.

He didn't argue.

But Dana could feel it—the exhaustion creeping in, the weight of too much, too fast pressing down on him.

He wasn't supposed to be here. The world was trying to take him back. And Dana wasn't going to let it.

A sharp crack echoed through the trees.

Dana gasped.

Caleb stumbled, his balance faltering for half a second.

"Shit—"

Dana yanked him up.

"Don't stop," she hissed.

He gritted his teeth, pushing forward, but Dana could see the signs. The strain. The way he was starting to slow. Then—

The light changed.

Dana's breath shuddered.

They were running—but the trees weren't moving right. The branches should have blurred past them, their surroundings shifting the way they always did when someone ran at full speed. But instead—They weren't changing at all. Everything looked exactly the same. No matter how far they ran, no matter how many steps they took—

The trees ahead were the same trees they had passed seconds ago. Like they were trapped in a loop. Like they weren't running anywhere at all.

Dana's stomach dropped.

Caleb must have seen it too because he swore under his breath.

"What the hell—"

He stopped, chest heaving, turning in a slow circle.

"This—this isn't right."

Dana's jaw tightened.

They had run. They had covered distance. So why were they still here? Why hadn't the forest changed? Then—a sound.

A whisper. But not a voice. Something older. The wind—not moving, but speaking.

And for the first time, Dana realized—

The Watchers weren't just chasing them. They were playing with them.

Dana's chest burned.

Not just from running. From the realization sinking in. They weren't getting anywhere. The trees weren't changing. They were running in circles. No—not circles. The forest itself was holding them in place. Like it was bending around them. Like it was watching them struggle and letting them wear themselves out.

Caleb's breath was sharp and uneven.

He turned again, his boots scraping against the dirt. His fingers curled into fists, frustration bleeding into his voice.

"This isn't possible," he muttered.

Dana swallowed. It didn't have to be possible. It just had to be happening.

Caleb pressed a hand to his head.

Dana caught the flicker of something on his face—not panic. Something worse. A shadow of recognition. Like he had been here before. Then—his body tensed.

Dana stepped forward. "Caleb?"

Caleb shook his head, sharp, rigid.

"No, no, I remember this," he muttered, voice rough. "This is how they keep you from leaving."

Dana's pulse spiked.

Caleb looked up at her, something dark in his eyes.

"This is what they did before they took me."

Dana's stomach dropped.

Caleb pressed his fingers to his temple, breathing hard.

"I ran. I ran just like this."

His voice was breaking, splintering under the weight of something clawing its way back.

"And every time—the road didn't come. The trees never changed."

Dana gritted her teeth.

This wasn't an accident. The Watchers were repeating the pattern. They were forcing him into the same moment again. Like a trap resetting itself. Like he was never supposed to escape.

Then—a sound.

Soft. Too close.

Dana's blood ran cold.

Not from the trees. Not from behind. From right beside them. A breath.

Caleb stiffened. His shoulders went rigid.

Dana slowly turned her head. And saw it.

A figure. Standing inches away.

Not approaching. Not moving.

It was just there.

Still. Watching.

Waiting.

Dana's hand shot out, gripping Caleb's wrist. Her throat was too tight.

Caleb barely breathed.

And then—

The thing smiled.

The smile was wrong. Not natural. Not human. Something in its shape—too sharp, too wide, like it didn't belong on a face.

They both staggered back.

And then—

Everything went black.

No sound. No wind. No trees. Just nothing.

Dana's pulse pounded.

Her body felt untethered.

Weightless. Like she had been pulled out of the world itself.

Her hands **searched for something—anything**—but found only void.

No ground. No sky. No Caleb. Then—

A whisper.

Soft. All around her. And then—inside her.

"Come back."

A lurch. A sensation like falling and being pulled at the same time. Her stomach twisted, her lungs seized—

And then—

Light.

Too bright. Too sudden.

Dana's knees buckled.

She slammed onto solid ground. A gasp ripped from her throat. The world snapped back into place.

Caleb hit the ground beside her. His body shook. His fingers twitched like something had crawled under his skin.

Dana tried to move. Her vision blurred. But she forced herself to focus.

And that's when she realized—

They weren't in the woods anymore. They were somewhere else.

Somewhere they shouldn't be.

Chapter 8

The first thing Dana felt was cold stone.

Damp. Unforgiving. Pressed against her cheek.

She inhaled sharply, her lungs aching, her fingers twitching against rough ground.

Her body was still shaking.

Not from cold. From whatever had just happened.

She forced her eyes open.

And saw nothing.

Darkness.

Not just the absence of light—something deeper.

Something that felt wrong.

Her breath came fast, shallow. She reached forward, fingers scraping against uneven rock—cold and slick with moisture, the rough edges biting into her skin.

The air smelled stale. Earthy.

Not the woods.

Not Pine Hollow.

Underground.

A sound.

Not loud.

Just the faintest scrape of movement.

Then—a voice.

"Dana."

Caleb.

His voice was strained.

Like he was fighting off a nightmare.

She turned toward the sound.

And in the darkness—a shape moved.

Dana crawled toward the sound.

Her palms scraped against the stone, damp and uneven beneath her fingers.

Somewhere ahead, Caleb shifted.

A sharp inhale. A ragged exhale.

He wasn't far. But she still couldn't see him.

The darkness here wasn't normal.

It was thick, pressing in like a living thing.
Like it had weight.
Her fingers brushed against fabric.
Caleb flinched.
She felt it in the way his body tensed beneath her touch.
"Caleb," she whispered.
His breathing was still too uneven.
She could hear it, the way he was struggling.
Then—his fingers twitched against hers.
"I'm here," he muttered, voice hoarse.
Dana exhaled.
She wasn't alone.
But that meant neither was he.
Because wherever they were, something had put them here.
And that something was still watching.
A flicker of light—faint at first, then pulsing, as if alive.
Faint. Wrong.
Not from above. Not from any source she could see.
It didn't chase the darkness away—it carved through it.
Thin slashes of sickly, shifting glow, seeping through the cracks in the walls like the veins of something buried alive.
Caleb sucked in a sharp breath.
Dana turned toward him, but he wasn't looking at her.
He was staring at the walls.
His expression unreadable.
Then, softly—
"…I've seen this before."
Caleb stared at the walls.
At the pulsing, unnatural glow seeping through the cracks in the stone.
Not like light—like something alive.
Caleb stood motionless.
His breath shallow, sharp.
His hands curled into fists at his sides.
And Dana saw it in his eyes.
The weight of full remembrance.
Not broken fragments. Not half-forgotten echoes.
The Watchers had tried to take everything from him.
But now—it was back.
And Dana knew, without a doubt—

The light had done it.
She didn't say it.
Didn't ask.
Because the way Caleb stood there, rigid and shaking, said enough.
Dana's voice was careful. "What did you remember?"
Caleb exhaled, but it was uneven.
He didn't look at her. Not right away.
His fingers twitched at his sides, his jaw tight.
And then—softly, but without hesitation—
"Everything."
Dana's stomach twisted.
She swallowed hard. "Caleb—"
"I wasn't supposed to leave," he murmured.
His voice was low. Distant.
Not broken. Steady.
"I was taken, Dana. But I wasn't the only one."
Dana's pulse spiked.
She already knew it.
But hearing him say it—it made it real.

Caleb's eyes finally met hers—wide, haunted, full of something raw and unsettled. Fear flickered beneath the surface, but there was something else, too. Determination. Like he had finally grasped something he wasn't willing to let go of again.

Something dark. Something deep.
And then—his words sent a chill through her.
"I remember where they are."
Dana stilled.
Her breath caught in her throat.
The walls around them seemed to close in.
Caleb's fingers twitched.
"The ones they took," he murmured.
"They're still there."

The light pulsed again—brighter, sharper. Dana felt it deep in her chest, an unnatural pull that made her want to move, to follow. Caleb flinched, his breath catching, as if the glow had reached inside him, stirring something he wasn't ready to face.

Brighter. Urging.
Like it wanted them to keep moving.
Dana exhaled sharply.
Caleb had been taken.
He had been erased.
But now he had come back.

And if his memories were right—

Maybe others could too.

Dana swallowed hard, forcing herself to focus. The path ahead of them was uneven, the pulsing glow carving eerie patterns into the walls. The air was thick, damp, carrying a weight that pressed against her skin.

Caleb took a slow step forward, then another. "If they're still there... we have to find them."

Dana nodded, though a whisper of doubt curled in her gut. The Watchers had let Caleb go. But why? And if the others were still trapped, what would they find when they reached them?

The glow brightened again, stretching deeper into the underground passage, beckoning them forward.

Dana inhaled sharply and followed.

The tunnel narrowed as they pressed forward, the damp air growing heavier, more oppressive. Each step sent echoes rippling through the stone passage, making it feel as if something unseen was moving alongside them—just out of reach.

Caleb moved with purpose now, his jaw tight, his posture rigid. The weight of his restored memories sat heavy on him, but he didn't hesitate. Whatever had been erased, whatever had been stolen, he had it back now. And he wasn't letting it go again.

The glow led them deeper, its pulsing rhythm steady, unwavering. A guide. A warning. Dana couldn't be sure which.

Then, ahead of them, the tunnel widened into something larger—a cavernous space where the glow pooled like liquid gold across the walls.

Caleb slowed.

Dana stepped up beside him, her pulse hammering.

Something was waiting for them in the dark.

A faint sound echoed through the cavern—distant, rhythmic, almost like breathing. The glow along the walls pulsed in response, stretching shadows into unnatural shapes. Dana tightened her fists, her skin prickling with unease.

Caleb inhaled sharply. "Do you hear that?"

Dana nodded, swallowing hard. The air had changed again, heavier, pressing down on them as if the underground itself was alive. Whatever was ahead, it wasn't just waiting.

It was aware of them.

Dana's fingers twitched at her sides, her instincts screaming to turn back, to run. But the glow urged them forward, and the cavern stretched before them like a gaping mouth waiting to swallow them whole.

Caleb clenched his jaw, taking a hesitant step forward. The rhythmic sound deepened, reverberating through the walls, vibrating beneath their feet.

Then—a shadow moved. Not against the walls, but within them. A figure, shifting just beneath the surface of the glowing stone, like something struggling to break free.

"Caleb—"

The glow pulsed wildly, flickering in uneven waves, casting their surroundings into moments of darkness. And in those blackened gaps, she saw them.

Figures. Dozens of them. Their shapes barely distinguishable from the stone itself.

Trapped.

Caleb exhaled sharply, his hand instinctively reaching for the wall but stopping just short of touching it. "They're still alive," he murmured. "Or... something close to it."

Dana's stomach twisted. The figures within the stone weren't moving—not yet—but something about them felt unfinished, like they were in a state of waiting. Not quite gone. Not quite here.

The glow pulsed again, illuminating the cavern in a brief, eerie flash. One of the shapes twitched.

Dana jerked back. "Caleb—"

Before she could finish, the rhythmic sound—the one that had been so distant before—shifted.

It wasn't just breathing anymore.

It was whispering.

Caleb stiffened beside her, his fingers twitching at his sides. His breath shallowed, his eyes locked onto the shifting figures. And then, in the dim, pulsing glow, his expression changed.

Recognition.

"Dana... I know them."

Dana's heart clenched. "What?"

Caleb swallowed hard. "They're not just anyone. I—I've seen them before. Before I was taken. Some of them were already here." He hesitated, his voice dropping to a whisper. "Some of them—they came after me."

Dana's skin prickled. The glow flickered again, illuminating the frozen faces beneath the surface of the stone. And for the first time, Dana saw it too.

The figures weren't strangers.

Dana's breath caught. Her pulse pounded in her ears as she scanned the faces, her gaze darting between them, searching—hoping. She took a slow step forward, her hand hovering inches from the stone.

Morgan.

The name formed in her mind before she could stop it. Her chest tightened as she searched the trapped figures, willing herself to find the face she had never stopped seeing in her nightmares. If Caleb had been here—if he had come back—then maybe, just maybe, Morgan was here too.

The glow pulsed again, shifting shadows across the stone. Dana's breathing stopped as a familiar shape flickered at the edge of her vision.

A face.

Half-buried. Half-lost.

Morgan.

They were familiar.

Dana took a step closer, her fingers trembling as they hovered just inches from the surface of the stone. The glow pulsed, illuminating the trapped figures in brief, flickering flashes. Her breath came uneven, her heartbeat a frantic drum in her chest.

Morgan.

She could see her now—faint, barely visible beneath layers of rock and shifting light. Her face was frozen in a moment of time, eyes open but empty, lips parted like she had been calling out before the stone swallowed her whole.

Dana's stomach twisted. "Morgan..." her voice cracked on the name, a whisper barely louder than the unnatural hum around them.

Caleb's breath was tight beside her. "Dana, don't—"

But she didn't hear him. Her palm pressed against the stone, and the glow flared violently.

A sharp jolt shot through Dana's arm the moment her skin met the stone. It wasn't just cold—it was alive, pulsing beneath her fingertips like something breathing, something aware. A low vibration crawled up her arm, spreading through her chest like a deep, unnatural hum. The glow intensified, wrapping around her hand, seeping into her skin.

Caleb swore, reaching for her, but the moment he tried to pull her back, a force threw him backward. He hit the ground hard, the impact knocking the breath from his lungs. Dana's eyes widened in alarm, but she couldn't move—her body was locked in place, tethered to the stone. The pulsing light had her now, and it was pulling.

The whispers rose. Not just one voice—many. Hundreds, maybe more, layered atop each other in a chaotic, echoing storm. They weren't words Dana could understand, but they wanted something from her. They wanted her to listen. She clenched her teeth, trying to pull back, but her fingers were sinking into the stone, her vision warping as the glow expanded around her.

The glow swallowed her whole.

For a moment, there was nothing—just weightlessness, just the distant hum of the voices surrounding her like a shroud. Dana couldn't see, couldn't feel the ground beneath her feet, couldn't tell if she was still standing or if she had been pulled into something else.

Then—snap.

The world slammed back into focus, and Dana wasn't in the cavern anymore.

She gasped, stumbling forward, her feet meeting soft earth instead of stone. The air was different—cool, damp, filled with the scent of pine and something burning. The unnatural glow was gone, replaced by the dim silver of moonlight filtering through trees.

She was in the woods.

Not just any woods.

The Pine Hollow woods.

Somewhere behind her, the whispering still murmured through the trees, but it was quieter now, stretched thin, as if it had been following her from somewhere far away. Dana turned sharply, her heart hammering against her ribs, searching the shadows.

And then—

A figure.

Standing just ahead, barely visible between the trees.

Dana's breath caught. Her stomach twisted with recognition, with a hope she didn't dare allow herself to feel.

Morgan.

Dana's chest tightened as she took a slow, hesitant step forward. "Morgan?" Her voice came out hoarse, barely more than a whisper. The figure didn't move at first. The moonlight barely touched her, but Dana could make out the unmistakable shape of long, tangled hair, the familiar slope of her shoulders. It was Morgan—it had to be.

But something was wrong.

Morgan stood too still, her posture too rigid, as if she weren't breathing. The shadows clung to her unnaturally, curling around her edges, keeping her face just out of reach. And when she finally did move, it was slow, unnatural—her head tilting in a way that sent a shudder through Dana's spine.

Dana swallowed hard, forcing herself to take another step closer. Her body screamed at her to stop, to turn back, but her mind refused to let go of the possibility—the hope—that this was real. That Morgan was real. That after all these years, after all the missing pieces, she had found her again.

"Morgan, it's me," Dana said, her voice steadier now, though her pulse hammered against her ribs. "It's Dana."

For a moment, nothing. Just the whisper of the wind through the trees, the lingering scent of burning pine. Then—a shift. Morgan's shoulders twitched, a slow, unnatural movement, like something adjusting itself inside a body that no longer quite fit. The shadows over her face thinned, just enough for Dana to see her eyes.

They were wrong.

Morgan's eyes weren't hers. They were hollow—not empty, but filled with something that didn't belong. Darkness swirled within them, moving like smoke trapped behind glass. There was no recognition, no spark of the best friend Dana had once known. Just void.

Dana's stomach twisted, and her fingers curled into fists. *No. No, this isn't right.* She had spent years holding on to the memory of Morgan, to the sound of her laughter, the way she used to roll her eyes at Dana's terrible jokes. This thing—this version of Morgan—wasn't her. It couldn't be.

Then Morgan moved.

Not a step forward. Not a twitch. But a glide, smooth and unnatural, her feet barely touching the ground as she closed the distance between them. The whispering in the trees grew louder, curling around Dana's ears, slithering into her thoughts.

"You found me."

Dana froze. The voice—it was Morgan's. But it didn't sound like it was coming from her lips. It was inside Dana's head, echoing from somewhere deeper, somewhere wrong.

Her pulse spiked.

"You found me... but you shouldn't have."

Morgan's lips finally moved, parting slightly, but the words still didn't come from her mouth. Her expression didn't change, her face still locked in that eerie, frozen almost-smile.

The whispering intensified, and the air grew heavier, pressing in against Dana's ribs. She staggered back, her breath coming too fast, panic tightening its grip around her throat.

Then—another voice.

"Dana!"

Caleb.

The moment she turned toward the sound of his voice, Morgan lunged.

Dana barely had time to react.

A flash of movement—a blur of shadow and pale skin—and Morgan was on her, fingers like ice-cold vices clamping around Dana's wrists. The force of the impact sent them both crashing to the ground, dirt kicking up around them as Dana struggled against the unnatural strength pressing her down.

Morgan's face was too close, her empty, swirling eyes staring through Dana rather than at her. Her grip burned like frostbite, her fingers digging into Dana's skin as if trying to hold her in place.

"You shouldn't have come," Morgan's voice rasped, inside Dana's head, seeping into her thoughts like smoke.

Dana clenched her teeth, fighting against the pressure. "You're not real," she hissed, twisting her body to try to break free. "You're not Morgan!"

Morgan's expression didn't change. Not anger, not sorrow—just emptiness. And then, her lips curled into a whisper of a smile.

"Not anymore."

A shockwave of cold exploded from Morgan's hands, surging up Dana's arms like ice water rushing through her veins. Memories flickered at the edges of her mind—but not her own. Morgan's.

A dark sky. A hand pulling her into the trees. The sound of her own voice screaming Dana's name. The moment the world went silent.

Dana's vision blurred. Her head pounded. The cold was spreading, pulling her under, trying to drown her in something she wasn't meant to see.

The shadows around Morgan stretched, her body flickering between solid and insubstantial, her limbs shifting unnaturally, like something was wearing her form rather than being her.

Then—Caleb moved.

He ripped Dana back, his grip firm as he yanked her away from Morgan's reach. The second their skin broke contact, the cold vanished, like snapping free from an undertow. Dana gasped, stumbling against him, her legs weak.

Morgan tilted her head, watching them. The whispering surged again, rising to a fever pitch, curling into Dana's thoughts like tendrils of smoke.

"You found me… but you shouldn't have."

Then—her form wavered.

Her body rippled, shadows peeling away in unnatural waves, distorting the space around her like a mirage. Then, with a final flicker, she vanished.

The whispering stopped instantly.

Silence crashed down around them, thick and suffocating.

Caleb didn't let go of Dana's arm, his breath coming fast, his fingers still tight where he'd pulled her back. "Dana," he said, his voice hoarse. "Are you okay?"

She swallowed hard, staring at the empty space where Morgan had been.

"She was here."

Caleb's jaw tightened. "That wasn't Morgan."

Dana's hands curled into fists, her nails digging into her palms. He was right.

It hadn't been Morgan.

But it had worn her like a mask.
And that meant one thing—Morgan Reece wasn't just taken.
She was still out there.
And whatever had her wasn't done yet.

Chapter 9

The woods were silent.

Not peaceful—unnatural.

Dana stood frozen, her breath coming in short, uneven bursts, her skin still tingling from the last remnants of the cold that Morgan—or what was left of her—had forced into her veins. The empty spot where Morgan had disappeared was still thick with something unseen, an absence that felt heavier than a presence.

Caleb was beside her, his own breathing sharp, his posture rigid. He hadn't spoken since pulling Dana away. He was staring at the trees like he expected them to move, like he was waiting for something else to step forward from the shadows.

Dana swallowed hard. Her voice came out quieter than she meant. "That wasn't her."

Caleb let out a slow breath through his nose. "No."

Silence stretched between them, thick with everything they weren't saying.

Then—the light flickered again.

The same unnatural glow that had pulsed through the underground walls twitched at the edges of the trees. Faint, subtle—barely there. But Dana saw it. Guiding. Leading.

She took a slow step forward. "We need to follow it."

Caleb didn't argue.

He just followed.

They moved carefully through the trees, the glow flickering just ahead, never quite within reach, but never far enough to lose sight of. It pulsed softly, like a heartbeat, threading through the undergrowth, guiding them deeper into the forest.

The air changed as they walked—denser, heavier. It smelled of damp earth and old wood, but underneath that, there was something else—something metallic, like the sharp tang of rusted iron.

Dana kept her eyes forward, but she could feel Caleb's tension beside her. He hadn't spoken since they started following the light, but she could hear it in his movements—the way his footsteps hesitated, the way his breath hitched just slightly every few minutes.

Then, he finally broke the silence.

"This isn't just leading us anywhere." His voice was low, steady, but there was something buried beneath it. Something he wasn't saying.

Dana glanced at him. "Then where?"

Caleb's jaw tightened. His eyes flickered to the trees. "It's leading us back."

Dana frowned, her steps faltering. "Back where?"

Caleb exhaled through his nose, gaze locked on the path ahead. "Think about it," he muttered. "Everything that's happened—the motel, the café, the Reeces… Every time we push forward, something tries to pull us back."

Dana's pulse quickened. He wasn't wrong. The patterns were there—leading them in circles, twisting their steps, keeping them tangled in the past instead of pushing toward anything new. But the glow—it wasn't pulling them away from something.

It was leading them toward something.

And then she saw it.

Through the trees, barely visible through the shifting dark—a house.

Her stomach dropped.

Her mother's house.

Dana had been back to the house before—but this time was different.

The first time, she had felt like an intruder in her own past, stepping through the remnants of her mother's life. The second, she had searched for answers, pushing back against the growing sense that something was watching. Now, as the glow pulsed at the edges of the frame, the house didn't feel like a place she had once known.

It felt like a threshold.

Caleb hovered at her side, his fingers twitching at his sides, but he didn't say anything as Dana reached for the door. The knob was ice-cold beneath her palm, the sensation sinking into her skin, making her hesitate for just a fraction of a second.

Then, she pushed it open.

The house exhaled around her, the air inside stale, heavy. The glow didn't follow them in—but it didn't need to.

Because something else was already here.

The moment Dana stepped inside, the air thickened, pressing against her skin like a weighted blanket. It was colder than it should have been. The house had always been quiet, always carried the weight of absence, but this was something else.

Caleb followed close behind, his steps cautious. "It feels different," he muttered, scanning the room.

Dana nodded. It did.

She had been here before, more than once—but now, standing in the dim, something had changed. The house felt less like a home and more like a space waiting to be filled. As if whatever had been watching her before wasn't just watching anymore.

Then, from down the hall—a sound.

A whisper. Faint. Just barely there.

Dana's pulse spiked. Her eyes snapped toward the hallway, where the darkness seemed deeper than it should be.

Caleb stiffened beside her. He had heard it too.

And then, softly, impossibly—her mother's voice.

"Dana."

Dana's breath caught in her throat.

She knew it wasn't real. It couldn't be. But the voice—it sounded exactly like her mother. The way Evelyn used to say her name, quiet but firm, like she was about to scold her for something.

Caleb took a step closer, his posture tense. "That's not her," he murmured.

Dana swallowed hard. "I know."

But her feet still moved forward.

The hallway stretched before her, the dim light from the living room failing to reach the end. The whisper had come from there—from her mother's bedroom.

She hesitated in the doorway. The room was as she had left it the last time she'd searched through her mother's things. The bed was neatly made, the curtains slightly parted, moonlight spilling over the floor. Nothing looked out of place.

But the whisper had come from here.

And then—the closet door creaked open.

Dana's stomach twisted.

She had checked that closet before. More than once. She had stood in this very spot, searching for anything—anything at all—that her mother might have left behind. And yet, as the door slowly creaked open, it felt as if she had never really looked at it before.

Caleb was right behind her, silent but ready.

The air in the room shifted, colder now. Dana could see her breath misting in front of her. The closet door hung open just enough to reveal darkness beyond it—deeper than the room itself, deeper than it should be.

A familiar instinct kicked in—she should turn back.

But before she could, something inside moved.

A slow, deliberate shift. A presence just beyond the threshold.

Then—her mother's voice again.

"You were never supposed to remember."

Dana's pulse pounded in her ears.

She knew it wasn't her mother. She knew. But the voice—it was perfect. The cadence, the weight behind the words, the way it pressed against her like a memory she wasn't sure she'd lived or dreamed.

Caleb moved beside her, barely a whisper of sound, but she could feel his tension. His breath was shallow, controlled—but his hand hovered near her arm, ready to pull her back if needed.

The closet door swung open further.

The darkness inside wasn't just darkness anymore.

Something shifted inside. Not stepping forward, not leaving the threshold—but waiting.

Dana clenched her fists, steadying herself. "Who are you?" she asked, her voice low, firm.

For a moment—nothing.

Then, softly, the voice answered.

"You already know."

Dana's throat went dry.

She had heard those words before. At the Reeces' house. The same eerie certainty, the same unsettling finality. But hearing it now, here, in her mother's house? It settled like ice in her chest.

Caleb's fingers brushed her wrist, a silent question. Do we run?

Dana didn't move.

She took a slow, measured breath and stepped closer.

The shadows inside the closet twisted, shifting like something half-formed, something waiting for the right moment to take shape. A breathy exhale echoed from the darkness.

Then, something reached out.

Not a hand—not exactly. Something longer, thinner, stretching toward her.

Dana jerked back, heart hammering, but the shadow didn't lunge.

It simply touched the doorframe—just lightly—before pulling back.

And when it did, something was left behind.

A photograph.

Dana stared at it.

It hadn't been there before.

But now it was.

She reached for it, her fingers brushing the edge of the aged paper, her breath catching as she turned it over.

It was a picture of her mother—young, maybe in her twenties. Standing in front of this very house.

And beside her—

Dana's stomach dropped.

Miriam.

Not just Miriam as Dana had always known her—older, distant, veiled in cryptic warnings.

But Miriam looking exactly the same as she did now.

She hadn't aged. Not at all.

Dana's grip on the photo tightened. Her pulse roared in her ears.

She turned to Caleb, her voice unsteady but certain.

"We need to find her."

Dana's fingers curled around the photograph, the weight of it too heavy for something so small. The image of her mother—young, smiling, unaware of what was coming—burned into her mind. But it was Miriam standing beside her that sent a deep, twisting unease through her chest.

Caleb shifted beside her, his eyes flicking from the photo to the darkness still lingering in the closet. "We're not staying here," he said firmly.

Dana swallowed hard. "I know."

They couldn't go back to the motel. The woods weren't safe. The town itself felt like a trap, tightening its grip the longer they stayed.

But there was one place that had answers—or at least, what was left of them.

"The library," Dana said, her voice steadier now. "The town records office is closed, but the library has archives. If Miriam's been around this long, there has to be something—something the Watchers haven't erased."

Caleb nodded. He didn't question it.

They needed to move. Before the Watchers decided to take something else.

The drive to the library was too quiet.

Dana gripped the photograph tightly in her lap, her thoughts racing. Her mother had known Miriam. Not just known her, but known her decades ago. And Miriam—she hadn't aged.

The implications churned in Dana's stomach.

What was Miriam, really?

Beside her, Caleb sat rigid in the passenger seat, his fingers tapping restlessly against his knee. The streetlights flickered as they passed, casting long, distorted shadows across the pavement. The town felt emptier than usual, like even the buildings were holding their breath.

Finally, Caleb spoke. "If Miriam's been here that long, what else is she hiding?"

Dana exhaled sharply. "That's what we're going to find out."

She turned into the library parking lot, the old brick building looming against the night. The town's archives were kept in the basement—a place no one really visited anymore.

As she put the car in park, movement near the entrance caught her eye.

A figure.

Standing just outside the glass doors.

Watching them.

Dana froze, her fingers tightening on the steering wheel.

The figure in front of the library stood perfectly still, just beyond the glass doors. Too still. At this distance, she couldn't make out the face—just a dark outline against the dim interior light.

Beside her, Caleb shifted. "Do you see that?"

Dana nodded slowly, her pulse steady but sharp. She forced herself to move, pushing open the driver's side door. The night air felt heavier now, thick with something unsaid.

Caleb stepped out beside her. His gaze flickered to the library entrance—then to the photograph still clutched in Dana's hand.

His breath caught.

Dana watched his reaction carefully. Caleb had already admitted he knew Miriam, but his expression now—**the way his body stiffened, the way his fingers twitched at his sides**—said something was clicking into place.

"You've seen this photo before," she said, more a statement than a question.

Caleb exhaled sharply, his fingers dragging through his hair. "No," he admitted. "But it makes sense now." His eyes flickered back to the dark figure inside. "She was always here, Dana. And I never questioned it."

The glass doors creaked open.

The figure inside stepped forward.

And the light from the library caught her face.

Miriam.

Waiting for them.

Dana's grip on the photograph tightened.

Miriam stood just inside the library entrance, her expression unreadable, her eyes sharp beneath the dim overhead light. She wasn't surprised to see them.

She had been waiting.

Caleb tensed beside Dana, his body rigid, his breath slow and measured. For a long moment, none of them moved. The air between them was thick with unspoken words.

Then Miriam tilted her head slightly, her voice calm but carrying an undeniable weight.

"You shouldn't be here."

Dana stepped forward. "We need answers." Her voice was steady, but inside, everything twisted.

Miriam didn't blink. "And what makes you think you're ready for them?"

Dana's stomach coiled with frustration. The cryptic warnings, the half-truths—she was done with it. She held up the photograph, her fingers digging into the edges.

"You knew my mother." Her voice wasn't a question.

Miriam's gaze flicked to Caleb, her expression hardening.

"You haven't changed," Caleb said, his voice edged with something sharp. "You were here before I was taken, and you're still here now. No different. No older. And I never thought to question it until now."

Miriam's posture stiffened.

"You never thought to question a lot of things," she said, her voice cool, clipped. "And yet here you are. Talking as if you have any claim to the truth."

Caleb's jaw tightened. "You could've stopped this. You could've—"

Miriam moved fast.

Not toward him—but forward just enough that the weight of her presence hit him like a wall. The air between them thickened, like a hand pressing against his chest.

"Watch your tone," she said softly, but there was nothing gentle about it. "You were a casualty of something far greater than you, and I do not owe you an explanation."

Caleb flinched, his breath hitching.

Dana stepped in before Caleb could recover. "Enough," she said, her voice sharp. She turned back to Miriam, her frustration boiling over. "I don't care what you are, what you know, or what you've done." She held up the photograph again, her grip tight. "But I know this—you were my mother's friend."

Miriam's expression didn't change, but Dana saw the faintest flicker of something behind her eyes.

"My mother trusted you," Dana pressed. "Did you ever trust her?"

A long silence. Then, Miriam exhaled slowly.

"I did," she said at last. "More than I should have."

The weight of those words settled between them.

Dana's pulse quickened. She had expected another deflection, another cryptic warning. But this—this was something real.

"Then prove it," she said, her voice steady. "Tell me the truth."

Miriam studied her for another long moment. Then, finally, she turned toward the dimly lit depths of the library.

"Come with me."

Dana and Caleb followed Miriam deeper into the library, the silence stretching between them like something alive. The overhead lights buzzed faintly, flickering in uneven pulses, casting long shadows across the rows of towering bookshelves.

Miriam led them toward the back, past the main reading area, past the old card catalog drawers, until she stopped at a narrow door marked "ARCHIVES." She pulled a key from inside her coat, unlocked it without hesitation, and pushed the door open.

A staircase spiraled downward into darkness.

Dana hesitated at the threshold. "How do you have a key to this place?"

Miriam gave her a look. "Do you really think a door is what keeps me out?"

Dana exhaled sharply but didn't argue.

Caleb, still tense from their earlier exchange, hovered just behind Dana, his silence heavy. Miriam had made it clear—she would tolerate Dana's attitude, but not his. He wasn't willing to test that boundary again.

Miriam started down the stairs first, her footsteps silent against the concrete steps. Dana followed, keeping her focus forward, ignoring the way the air changed as they descended.

It was colder here. Drier.

And when they reached the bottom, Dana understood why.

The walls weren't just lined with old town records.

They were lined with things that shouldn't exist.

Maps with locations that didn't appear on modern charts. Old newspaper clippings that had been deliberately removed from town archives. Pages of handwritten notes, scribbled in a frantic, uneven scrawl.

And in the center of the room—

A single wooden filing cabinet.

Miriam walked straight toward it, pressing a hand against the worn surface. For a moment, she didn't speak.

Then, softly—**almost reluctantly**—she said:

"Your mother wasn't just trying to protect you, Dana."

She turned to face her fully.

"She was trying to stop what's coming."

Dana's breath caught.

She had expected cryptic warnings, vague half-truths—but this wasn't that. This was something real. Something final.

Caleb stepped closer, his eyes flicking between Miriam and the filing cabinet. He wasn't breathing quite right. Like he could feel what was coming, but didn't know if he wanted to face it.

Dana swallowed hard. "What's coming?"

Miriam didn't answer immediately. Instead, she opened the cabinet.

The drawers slid out smoothly, too smoothly for something so old. Inside were files—dozens of them, yellowed with age, edges curling with time. Some were labeled with dates. Others had names.

Dana's stomach twisted as she scanned them. She knew these names.

People who had vanished. People no one remembered anymore.

Caleb reached out, hesitating before touching one of the folders. "They shouldn't exist," he murmured. "Not if the Watchers erased them."

Miriam glanced at him, her expression unreadable. "That's why they're here."

Dana reached for a file near the front, fingers brushing over the name written in faded ink. Morgan Reece.

Her chest tightened.

She pulled it out, opened it—

And the first thing inside was a photograph.

Not just of Morgan.

Of Morgan and Dana.

Together.

But something was wrong.

Dana didn't remember this picture being taken. Not just that—she didn't remember this version of Morgan.

Morgan's eyes weren't quite right.

Caleb looked over her shoulder, his breath hitching.

"That's not the Morgan I knew," he muttered.

Dana felt a slow chill creep down her spine.

Because she was starting to realize—

This wasn't a record of the missing.

It was a record of what the Watchers had changed.

Dana's fingers tightened around the photograph.

It was Morgan—but it wasn't.

The longer she stared at the image, the more she felt it—a wrongness buried in the details. Morgan's smile was just a little too stiff. The light in her eyes, the way she held herself, the angle of her head—it was close, but not quite real.

Caleb let out a slow breath beside her, his posture rigid. "What is this?"

Miriam watched them carefully. "A fracture," she said. "A piece of something that shouldn't exist anymore."

Dana swallowed. "You mean… this is something the Watchers erased."

Miriam's jaw tightened slightly, but she nodded. "Or rather—something they tried to erase."

Dana glanced back at the cabinet, her pulse pounding. If this wasn't just a list of the missing—but of **things the Watchers had altered**—then that meant…

There were still pieces left.

Fragments of memories, faces, moments that should have been wiped away.

Caleb exhaled sharply. "If these still exist… does that mean we can bring them back?"

Miriam's expression darkened.

"You're not supposed to be asking that question."

Dana snapped her gaze up to her. "But it's possible, isn't it?"

Miriam didn't answer. Not immediately.

Then—for the first time since they had met her—she looked uncertain.

Dana's chest tightened.

Caleb took a step closer. "Miriam."

Her eyes flicked to him, her patience thinning. "You think this is a game, don't you?" Her voice was sharper now. "You think you can just put things back the way they were, like time works in your favor."

Caleb's jaw tightened, but he didn't back down. "If there's a way to fix this—"

"Fix what, exactly?" Miriam snapped, stepping toward him. The air in the room shifted. "You think you're the first person to want to undo what's been done? That you're somehow different?"

Caleb flinched.

Dana stepped in, her voice hard. "Miriam."

Miriam's attention snapped back to her. The sharp edge of her presence recoiled slightly—not gone, but pulled back, contained.

Dana took a slow breath. "You said my mother was trying to stop what's coming." She held up the photograph. "What did she know?"

Miriam studied her, silent.

Then, finally, she exhaled.

"She knew the cycle had to be broken," she said quietly.

Caleb frowned. "Cycle?"

Miriam's gaze darkened. "You already know."

Dana's stomach twisted.

Because deep down—she did.

Everything that had happened, everything that was **happening now**—it had happened before.

And it would keep happening.

Unless they stopped it.

Dana's fingers tightened around the edges of the photograph. The cycle had to be broken. That was what her mother had believed—what she had fought for. But the way Miriam said it—**the weight behind her words**—made something cold settle in Dana's chest.

Caleb took a slow step forward, his voice steady but edged with frustration. "Then how do we stop it?"

Miriam exhaled sharply, her gaze flicking between them. For the first time, she hesitated.

Dana pressed. "Miriam."

Finally, she spoke.

"You assume it can be stopped without consequence."

The air shifted, thickening again, but this time, it wasn't just the force of Miriam's presence. Something else stirred. The hum in Dana's ears—the feeling of being watched—tightened like invisible hands closing around her throat.

Caleb's posture stiffened. "What was that?"

Miriam's eyes flickered to the ceiling.

"We've been here too long."

Dana's pulse spiked.

Miriam moved fast, grabbing a handful of files—not all of them, just the ones she deemed important. She shoved them into Dana's hands.

"Take these. If you want to break the cycle, start with what's inside."

Dana barely had time to react before the library lights flickered violently. The hum rose into a whisper—not just one voice. Many.

Miriam turned sharply toward the staircase, her posture tense.

"They know we're here."

A pulse of cold air rushed through the room. The shadows along the walls stretched unnaturally.

Then—the basement door slammed shut.

Caleb moved first, yanking Dana back. "We need to go. Now."

Dana's heart pounded. The whispering was getting louder.

And then, from somewhere in the dark—

A voice too familiar to be real.

"Dana."

Her mother's voice.

But when Dana turned toward the sound—the shadows moved.

Dana's stomach dropped.

Her mother's voice—it was too perfect. Not distorted, not hollow, not distant like a memory—it was exactly as she remembered it. But her mother was dead.

The shadows in the room stretched, curling toward the corners of the ceiling, pressing against the bookshelves. Something was in here with them.

Caleb pulled at her wrist, his voice urgent. "Dana, don't—"

But she was already turning toward the voice.

And **for the briefest second**—she saw her.

Evelyn Crowell stood in the dim light between the bookshelves, just out of reach. Her expression was soft, her eyes warm in the way Dana had longed for since she died.

It looked like her.

But it wasn't.

Miriam moved faster than Dana had ever seen. In an instant, she was between them, an arm raised—not in defense, but in warning.

"Don't listen," Miriam hissed.

The moment she spoke, Evelyn's face shifted.

Not physically—not in the way flesh and bone move—but in something deeper. The warmth in her eyes flickered—not fading, but warping. The expression wasn't a mother's love. It was something else wearing her mother's face.

It wasn't her mother.

It was the Watchers.

The whispering grew louder. More voices. More faces. The shadows rippled, stretching like unseen hands reaching toward them.

Miriam didn't wait. She grabbed Dana by the collar and shoved her backward—hard.

"Run."

Dana hit the ground hard, her palms scraping against the cold concrete floor. The whispers surged, pressing against her skull like a storm of voices just on the edge of understanding.

Miriam didn't move back.

She stood firm between Dana and the shifting, half-formed thing wearing Evelyn Crowell's face. The Watchers weren't hiding anymore. They were testing. Pushing. Seeing how far they could reach.

Caleb grabbed Dana's arm, pulling her up. "We have to move—"

Miriam raised a hand. The entire room trembled.

The whispers faltered, a ripple through the darkness like a breath caught in a throat. The shadows near the shelves shrank back.

Dana's eyes widened.

Miriam wasn't just **blocking the Watchers' influence anymore**—she was forcing them back.

She took a slow step forward, and the thing in the shape of Evelyn twitched, its form blurring at the edges. The warmth in its eyes flickered—like a dying ember, like a mask slipping.

Miriam's voice was low, sharp as a blade.

"You cannot have them."

The whispering screamed.

The shadows lurched forward—but Miriam lifted both hands and the very air shuddered. The bookshelves rattled, the walls groaned, and something unseen buckled under her command.

A force pushed outward, slamming into the Watchers like a tidal wave. The false image of Evelyn disintegrated into nothing, ripped apart by something more powerful than it.

Dana's breath caught. The pressure was gone. The whispering had vanished.

And Miriam—Miriam was still standing, untouched.

But she looked furious.

She turned to Dana and Caleb, her expression carved from stone.

"They won't stop now."

Caleb exhaled shakily. "They weren't stopping before."

Miriam's gaze darkened. "You don't understand." She turned, grabbing the remaining files from the cabinet and shoving them into Dana's hands.

"Take these and go," she ordered.

Dana hesitated. "Miriam—"

Miriam's voice was low, dangerous.

"Go. Now."

The library lights flickered wildly overhead. The shadows were stirring again.

Dana didn't argue. She turned and ran.

Dana's feet pounded against the floor as she sprinted up the stairs, the files clutched tightly to her chest. Caleb was right behind her, his breath sharp and uneven, and behind them—the shadows were moving.

The whispering surged again, thick and layered, curling through the air like invisible hands reaching for them. The voices weren't speaking in words—they were scraping at the edges of Dana's mind, trying to pull something loose.

Miriam was last up the stairs, but she didn't run.

Dana risked a glance back—and saw the air around Miriam bend. The shadows lurched toward her, but they couldn't quite touch her, as if an invisible force was holding them back.

But they were testing her.

Dana turned forward just in time to hit the door at full speed. She slammed her shoulder into it, the old wood groaning before bursting open. Cold night air hit her like a shock, and she staggered forward into the parking lot.

Caleb was next, nearly tripping over himself, and then—Miriam.

The moment she crossed the threshold, the whispering stopped.

The library door slammed shut behind her.

Silence.

The weight pressing against Dana's skull vanished.

For a long moment, none of them moved. The wind whistled through the empty street, and the streetlights flickered like nothing had ever happened.

Caleb turned to Miriam, his breath still coming fast. "What the hell was that?"

Miriam didn't answer right away. She was staring at the library door, her jaw tight, her shoulders rigid.

Then, finally—she exhaled.

"They're growing impatient."

Dana swallowed, still clutching the files against her chest. "Because of us?"

Miriam's gaze flicked to her, something grim and knowing in her expression. "Because of what you're about to learn."

Dana's grip tightened on the files, the weight of Miriam's words settling like stone in her chest.

Because of what she was about to learn.

She exchanged a glance with Caleb, whose breathing was finally steadying. He was watching Miriam carefully, his jaw tight. "Then we need to move," he said, voice low. "We can't stay here."

Miriam didn't argue. She turned away from the library, already walking toward the darkened street. "Follow me."

Dana hesitated. "Where are we going?"

Miriam didn't stop. "Somewhere they won't find you immediately."

That didn't feel like much of a comfort, but Dana didn't question it. The Watchers had already found them everywhere else. If Miriam had a place where their reach was weaker—wherever that was—it was better than standing in an open parking lot waiting for them to strike again.

Dana moved quickly, falling into step behind her. Caleb followed, his posture tense, his gaze flicking to the darkened storefronts as if expecting something to step out of the shadows.

The wind picked up, rustling the trees that lined the quiet streets. The town felt off, even more than usual. Too still. Too expectant. Like it was watching them leave.

Dana shivered, pulling her jacket tighter around herself. "Where is this place?"

Miriam didn't look back.

"Somewhere only your mother and I knew."

Dana's pulse spiked at Miriam's words.

Somewhere only her mother and Miriam knew.

That meant this place mattered. It wasn't just a hiding spot—it was something Evelyn had kept secret. And if she had kept it secret, then the Watchers had a reason to fear it.

They walked quickly, the silence between them heavy, broken only by the wind threading through the streets. Caleb stayed close, his eyes flickering toward every alley, every shifting shadow, his body tense and ready.

Miriam led them past the last rows of buildings, away from the familiar streets, toward the outer edges of town. The air changed here—crisper, sharper. Not colder, but heavier, like the space itself carried a weight Dana couldn't place.

She knew where they were going before Miriam even stopped.

The woods.

Not the part that led to the old paths. Not where Morgan had disappeared.

Somewhere deeper. Somewhere Dana had never dared to go before.

Caleb exhaled sharply beside her. "Of course it's the woods," he muttered.

Miriam shot him a look. "You're welcome to stay behind."

Caleb didn't respond, but Dana could feel his frustration. It didn't matter. They weren't turning back now.

Miriam stepped into the trees, moving with purpose. Dana and Caleb followed.

The branches closed around them, swallowing them whole.

The deeper they walked into the trees, the heavier the air became. Not suffocating, but dense—charged, like the moment before a storm.

Dana kept her focus ahead, following Miriam's sure steps. She moved through the undergrowth like she had walked this path a thousand times, even though Dana couldn't see anything resembling a trail. The deeper they went, the more the forest felt wrong.

Not in the way the Watchers made it feel—not like something watching from the trees, pressing against the edges of her mind.

This was different. Older.

Caleb exhaled through his nose, keeping close to Dana's side. "How far are we going?"

Miriam didn't answer right away.

Then—softly, almost like a warning:

"Far enough that they won't follow."

The way she said it made Dana's skin prickle. Not "can't." "Won't."

Miriam slowed, stopping in a small clearing. The ground here was different. The grass grew taller, untouched. The air had a stillness that didn't belong.

And in the center of the clearing—

A circle of stones.

Weathered. Ancient. Half-buried in the earth.

Caleb muttered a curse under his breath. "Tell me this isn't some kind of—"

Miriam cut him off. "It's a threshold."

Dana's throat tightened.

"A threshold for what?"

Miriam turned to her then, studying her carefully.

"For those who were never meant to be forgotten."

Dana stared at the circle of stones, her chest tightening.

For those who were never meant to be forgotten.

She exhaled slowly, stepping closer. The stones weren't arranged naturally—they were placed. Purposeful. A marker, a barrier, a boundary.

Caleb tensed beside her, glancing at Miriam. "So what does that mean? What is this place?"

Miriam's gaze didn't leave the stones. "It's a tether."

Dana frowned. "A tether to what?"

Miriam finally looked at her, her expression unreadable. "To them."

The words sent a slow chill down Dana's spine.

The missing. The erased.

Morgan.

Ben.

Everyone the Watchers had taken.

Caleb swallowed. "You're saying—"

Miriam cut him off. "I'm saying this is the only place that still remembers them."

Dana's pulse pounded. She turned to the stones, staring at the center of the circle. The air inside felt... thinner. Like it wasn't just space, but something else.

Somewhere else.

Miriam exhaled, stepping toward her. "If you want to bring them back, this is where we start."

Dana's breath caught.

The Watchers erased people. Scrubbed them from existence, rewrote reality to make sure they were never remembered.

But if Miriam was right...

Then maybe they weren't completely gone.

Maybe they were just waiting to be found.

Dana's fingers curled into fists. If this place was a tether, a space where the erased still lingered, then maybe—just maybe—she could pull them back.

She stepped closer to the circle of stones, her pulse hammering. The air inside the boundary was different—not just still, but expectant. As if something was watching from just beyond the veil.

Caleb hesitated. "Dana—"

She crouched down, reaching out toward one of the stones. The moment her fingers brushed the surface, the entire clearing shifted.

Not physically. Not in any way she could see.

But the weight in the air thickened, pressing against her chest. The world around her felt like it had… tilted.

Caleb cursed under his breath. "What did you just do?"

Dana didn't answer. She was staring into the center of the circle, her breath shallow. Something was there.

Not a shape. Not a person.

But a presence.

A feeling.

The whispering started again—not like before, not the voices of the Watchers.

This was different. Familiar.

Dana's pulse spiked as a sound carried through the clearing—faint, distant, like an echo across time.

Her name.

Dana staggered back.

Caleb grabbed her arm, steadying her. "Dana—what was that?"

She shook her head, her vision swimming. The sound had been so soft. But she had heard it.

She knew that voice.

It was Ben.

Miriam stepped beside her, her expression unreadable.

"They're still here," Dana whispered.

Miriam's gaze darkened.

"For now," she said.

And somehow, Dana knew what she meant.

This place—the tether—it wasn't permanent.

The erased were still there, but if the cycle continued…

Eventually, even this place would forget them.

Dana swallowed hard, her mind spinning. The files Miriam had forced into her hands felt heavier now. If this place—the tether—was the last connection to those who had been erased, then whatever was in these documents had to be crucial.

Caleb crossed his arms, still staring at the circle of stones like it might bite him. "Alright," he said, shifting his weight. "So what now? Do we hold hands and chant, or do we just hope real hard?"

Miriam's head turned slowly.

Caleb barely had time to react before the air around him shifted. His shoulders stiffened—not from a touch, but from something unseen, like an invisible weight pressing just enough to remind him who was in charge.

Miriam's voice was flat, sharp. "Shut the fuck up."

Caleb blinked, hesitating just enough for Dana to watch him think through his next words carefully.

He took a single step back. "Right. Got it."

Dana exhaled, shaking her head. "Can we focus?"

Miriam turned back toward the tether, her expression serious once again. "There's no ritual," she said, "and no chanting. What we do next depends entirely on what's in those files." She nodded toward the stack in Dana's hands.

Dana stared down at them.

The names. The dates.

All the people the Watchers had erased.

All the people who still existed here, even in fragments.

She turned toward the stones. The air inside the circle was different. Thinner. Quieter. Waiting.

If there was a way to bring them back—

It started here.

Dana turned the first file over in her hands, fingers tracing the faded ink. Morgan Reece.

The paper felt too fragile, too thin for something that held what was left of a person. But here it was—a name that had been erased, a record that shouldn't exist.

She swallowed hard and pulled the file open.

Inside, there were fragments. Not full records, not official documents. Just scraps. A torn piece of a missing person's report. A school photo—Morgan, younger, smiling like she didn't know what was coming. Notes, handwritten but incomplete.

Dana frowned, scanning the scribbled words. Some of the ink had faded completely, like time itself had tried to erase them.

"Subject identified for removal. Expected transition: gradual.

Memory fractures appearing in close associates. No anomalies.

Cycle remains intact."

Her stomach twisted. "Identified for removal." The words felt clinical. Cold.

Like Morgan hadn't been a person at all—just another piece of the cycle.

Caleb read over her shoulder, his jaw tight. "It's like they were tracking it," he muttered. "Like they knew exactly how long it would take for everyone to forget her."

Dana exhaled sharply, flipping through the rest of the file. Nothing about where she was taken. Nothing about what happened to her after.

Just a process. A system.

She turned to Miriam. "How did this survive?"

Miriam studied the file for a moment before speaking. "Because your mother made sure it did."

Dana's breath caught.

She held the file tighter. "My mother—"

But before she could finish, something shifted in the clearing.

A flicker.

The whispering returned—not loud, not pressing. Just a single, frayed sound.

Dana's heart skipped.

It wasn't coming from the woods.

It was coming from inside the circle.

She turned toward the stones, pulse hammering.

And in the space between them—

A figure was forming.

Dana's breath caught.

The air inside the circle shimmered, bending like heat rising off pavement. But the temperature wasn't hot—it was cold. The kind of cold that settled in the bones, that pressed in from somewhere else entirely.

The whispering grew clearer.

Not a chorus. Not the layered, shifting voices of the Watchers.

Just one.

Dana stepped closer.

Caleb caught her wrist. "Dana—"

But she barely heard him.

Because the shape inside the stones was becoming clearer.

A figure—faint, wavering, like an old photograph coming into focus. Not whole, not entirely here. But there.

And Dana knew that silhouette.

Her stomach clenched. "Morgan."

The whispering stopped.

And Morgan—**or whatever was left of her**—lifted her head.

Her eyes met Dana's.

They weren't hollow like before.

They were tired.

Fading.

And then, softly—barely a breath—she spoke.

"You shouldn't be here."

Dana's chest tightened.

The last time she had seen Morgan—if she could even call it that—her voice had been wrong. Hollow. A mask of something else. But this? This was different.

This voice was hers.

Caleb tensed beside her. Dana could feel his grip hovering, like he was debating whether to pull her back. "Is that really her?" he asked, his voice low.

Miriam didn't answer immediately.

She was watching Morgan carefully, her expression unreadable.

Dana took a step closer. The image wavered, but didn't disappear.

Morgan's form wasn't whole. She looked **transparent, incomplete**—like a reflection in water. But her eyes… her eyes were sharp with recognition.

Dana swallowed hard. "Morgan?"

Morgan's lips parted slightly, like she wanted to say something. But then—she flinched.

Her entire form rippled, distorting violently, her features twisting in pain.

Dana lunged forward on instinct. "Morgan—"

Miriam's hand shot out, stopping her cold.

Dana gasped as something unseen slammed into her chest, pushing her back. It wasn't a shove—it was a force, something without hands, without a body, but undeniable.

She stumbled, her breath catching as Morgan's entire form flickered.

And then, the whispering returned.

Stronger this time. Not just Morgan.

Something else.

Miriam's voice cut through the air—sharp and commanding. "Step back. Now."

Dana didn't move.

Morgan's **mouth opened like she was screaming**—but no sound came out.

Then, she looked at Dana.

And her expression shifted.

Not fear. Not pain.

But warning.

"They're coming."

The clearing lurched.

The whispering surged into a roar.

And the trees came alive.

The trees shuddered, their branches twisting, reaching. The air turned thick and suffocating, like the entire forest had shifted against them.

Dana's pulse spiked. The whispering wasn't just coming from Morgan anymore. It was everywhere.

Miriam's stance hardened.

She didn't just step between Dana and Morgan—she anchored herself, like she was holding something back. The space around her rippled, warping the way it had back in the library.

Caleb grabbed Dana's arm, pulling her back. "We need to go. Now."

But Dana couldn't move. She couldn't leave Morgan.

Morgan's form was flickering now, her expression strained. She was still trying to say something.

Dana took a desperate step forward. "Morgan, tell me how to—"

Morgan's head snapped up. Her eyes widened.

And then—she was gone.

Vanished.

Not slowly. Not like before.

She was ripped away.

Like something had yanked her back into the void.

Dana gasped, her chest tightening like a fist had closed around it.

Then—a shadow moved behind the trees.

Not flickering. Not shifting.

Something solid. Watching. Waiting.

The whispering turned to laughter.

Not human. Not real.

Something else.

Miriam's voice was sharp, unyielding. "RUN."

Dana didn't hesitate.

She turned and bolted from the clearing.

Dana's feet pounded against the forest floor, her breath ragged as she ran. The whispering chased them, curling through the trees like invisible hands, too close, too eager.

Caleb was right beside her, his movements quick, precise. He didn't waste breath asking what had happened—he had seen enough.

But Dana's mind was still racing.

Morgan had been there. Real. A fragment. She had recognized Dana. Warned her.

And then—she was gone.

Ripped away.

Like the Watchers had been waiting.

Like they had been listening.

Miriam was the last to move, but she caught up effortlessly, her presence steady behind them. She didn't run like they did—she moved like the forest was bending to let her pass.

Dana glanced back, her chest tightening. The clearing was already gone, swallowed by the dark. The trees **looked the same in every direction now**—twisting, looming, stretching high above, blotting out the sky.

No paths. No landmarks.

Caleb swore under his breath. "Where the hell are we going?"

Miriam didn't slow. "Away from them."

The whispering spiked, splitting into too many voices. Some were familiar—faces Dana had known, people who had been erased.

But others—others weren't.

They weren't names she knew.

They weren't voices she had ever heard.

And that scared her more.

Caleb reached out, grabbing Dana's arm again. "Dana, don't listen."

Miriam suddenly stopped.

Dana almost collided with her. "What—"

Miriam lifted a hand, palm open. The air in front of them stilled.

Then—something passed through the trees ahead.

Not a shadow. Not a flicker.

Something tall. Solid. Watching.

Waiting.

Dana's stomach dropped.

The whispering stopped.

Everything stopped.

And then—

It took a step toward them.

Dana's breath caught.

The figure ahead of them—it wasn't fading, wasn't shifting like the Watchers she had seen before. It was solid. Defined. Like it had always been there, waiting for them to notice.

Miriam didn't move, didn't speak. But Dana could feel the shift in her presence. The way the air around her tensed, as if she was bracing for something.

Caleb exhaled sharply. "That's not one of the usual ones, is it?"

Miriam's voice was flat. Unreadable.

"No."

The figure took another step forward.

It was tall, its form just barely visible between the trees. Not fully illuminated, but not hidden either. The way light bent around it was unnatural, swallowing the space where its features should have been.

But the worst part—

It wasn't whispering.

All the other Watchers—they whispered, they layered themselves in voices, they crawled into the spaces between thoughts and twisted memory like a blade.

This one didn't.

It didn't need to.

Because Dana already knew what it was.

She had seen it before.

Not fully—just flickers, at the edge of her vision. A presence that had always felt different from the others.

And now—it was here.

Watching.

Waiting.

For her.

Miriam moved first.

She lifted a hand—not a warning this time, but something sharper. A command.

The air cracked. The pressure slammed outward, the trees shuddering as something unseen forced the space between them wider.

Caleb stumbled back. "What the—"

Miriam's voice was low. Dangerous.

"Run."

But Dana couldn't move.

Because the figure—the thing standing before them—

Didn't flinch.

Didn't react.

Just took another step forward.

Miriam's jaw tightened.

And for the first time since Dana had met her—

She looked afraid.

Dana's pulse pounded in her ears.

Miriam was afraid.

She had seen Miriam angry, frustrated, annoyed beyond belief at Caleb—but never this. Never genuinely afraid.

The thing in the trees—it wasn't stopping.

It moved with certainty. Unhurried. Like it knew it had all the time in the world.

Caleb grabbed Dana's arm, pulling her back. "Dana, we have to go. Now."

Miriam's posture hardened. The space around her rippled again, but Dana could see it—this thing wasn't backing down.

Miriam had forced Watchers back before. This one wasn't listening.

It wasn't just any Watcher.

It was something worse.

Miriam exhaled sharply, her hands curling at her sides.

"I told you to run," she muttered.

Dana snapped out of it—her instincts finally kicking in. She turned and bolted.

Caleb was already moving, and for the first time, Miriam didn't lead the way.

She stayed behind.

Holding it back.

The forest blurred around Dana as she ran, her breath burning in her chest. The whispering never returned.

The Watchers weren't chasing them.

Because they didn't need to.

Something far worse was already here.

Chapter 10

Dana didn't stop running until the trees thinned and the pressure in the air eased.

Her lungs burned, her legs ached, but she didn't dare slow down. Not until she was sure they had put enough distance between themselves and whatever that thing was.

Caleb kept pace beside her, his breath coming fast. Neither of them spoke. The weight of what had just happened pressed in too heavy, too immediate.

They had left Miriam behind.

Dana's stomach twisted at the thought, but there had been no other choice.

Miriam had told them to run. Had stayed behind to face that thing alone.

And Dana didn't know if she was coming back.

The thought sent a fresh jolt of panic through her, but she forced herself to keep moving. Miriam had made her choice. Now Dana had to figure out what the hell to do next.

The trees gave way to open road. Dana barely registered where they were before Caleb grabbed her wrist, forcing her to stop.

She turned sharply. "Caleb, we have to—"

But he was staring at her.

His expression wasn't panic, or frustration. It was something else.

Something cold.

Something like recognition.

Dana's breath caught.

"What?" she asked, her voice barely steady.

Caleb didn't blink.

"Dana... I remember."

Dana froze.

Caleb's words hung in the air, cutting through the lingering panic still crawling up her spine.

"Dana... I remember."

She turned to him sharply, her pulse hammering. "What do you mean you remember?"

Caleb's expression was tight, his breathing still uneven from the run. But there was something else in his eyes—something raw, something real.

"I mean it's back," he said, swallowing hard. "All of it."

Dana's stomach twisted.

Caleb had been taken—erased. And when he came back, his memory was fractured. Pieces missing. Things lost to whatever the Watchers had done to him.

But now—

Now, he was saying it was all back.

Dana clenched her jaw. "How?"

Caleb shook his head. "I don't know. But when we ran—when she told us to run—it was like something snapped." His fingers twitched at his sides. "Like something stopped holding it back."

Dana's grip on the files tightened.

This wasn't just about the thing Miriam tried to stop.

It wasn't just about what happened to her.

Something had changed.

Dana shook her head. "That doesn't make sense. The Watchers don't just give memories back. If they could, they wouldn't have erased you in the first place."

Caleb shook his head quickly. "They didn't give me anything back. I think… something snapped." He swallowed hard. "Like whatever was keeping me from remembering just… stopped working." His voice lowered. "Like they're losing control."

Dana felt a chill run through her.

She had been so focused on breaking the cycle, on fighting back, on resisting. But if the cycle was breaking already—if something had shattered before they were ready for it—

What would happen next?

Caleb let out a harsh breath. "And, Dana—" He turned toward her, his eyes sharp, haunted. "I wasn't alone when they took me."

Dana's breath caught.

"There were others."

The words sat heavy in the air, a truth too big to process all at once.

Caleb stared past her, his jaw clenched tight, his hands still curled into fists at his sides. His breath wasn't steady anymore.

Dana forced herself to speak. "Who?"

Caleb swallowed. "I don't know all their names." His voice was low, raw. "Some of them were already there when I was taken. Some… some came after."

Dana's pulse spiked.

After.

That meant—this wasn't just about the past.

People were still being taken.

Caleb dragged a hand through his hair, his eyes flicking toward the treeline, like he expected something to step out at any second. "I remember pieces of it. The place they kept us—it wasn't like this." He gestured to the forest, the roads, the real world around them. "It was… outside of time. Outside of everything."

Dana tightened her grip on the files. "What do you mean?"

Caleb exhaled sharply. "I mean, it wasn't just being erased. It was being stuck. I don't know how long I was there because time didn't work the same way." He looked back at her, something dark in his expression. "Dana, I haven't aged the way I should have."

The realization hit her like a fist.

Caleb had been gone for decades.

Over forty years.

But he hadn't changed.

She had seen fragments of this truth before—the way he didn't recognize new technology, how out of place he felt in a world that had moved on without him.

But this—this made it real.

Caleb let out a slow, unsteady breath. "They didn't just take us." His voice dropped lower. "They kept us."

Dana's stomach twisted.

She had always assumed the people who were erased were simply… gone.

But if Caleb was right—if they were taken, if they were held somewhere else—

Then maybe the others weren't lost.

Maybe they were still there.

Waiting.

Caleb exhaled sharply. "I mean, it wasn't just being erased. It was being stuck. I don't know how long I was there because time didn't work the same way." He looked back at her, something dark in his expression. "Dana, I haven't aged the way I should have."

Dana didn't flinch. "I know that."

Caleb shook his head. "No, you don't." His voice was sharper now, urgent. "I haven't aged because we weren't in time at all."

Dana's stomach turned.

Caleb's words weren't just about himself. If what he was saying was true—if time didn't touch the people who were taken—then the others…

Morgan.

All this time, she had assumed Morgan was gone. Erased.

But what if she wasn't?

What if she was still there—wherever Caleb had been—trapped outside of time, stuck in a place no one was supposed to remember?

Caleb's voice dropped lower. "They didn't just take us, Dana. They kept us."

The realization slammed into her.

They weren't just fighting against the erasures.

They were fighting for the ones who were still trapped.

Dana's breath shook.

If the erased weren't just gone—if they were still out there, waiting—then this wasn't just about breaking the cycle.

This was about getting them back.

She clutched the files tighter, her heartbeat hammering in her ears. "Where?"

Caleb frowned. "What?"

Dana turned to him sharply. "Where were you kept? If you were trapped somewhere, if time didn't move—where was it?"

Caleb swallowed, his gaze flickering, like he was trying to pull the answer from somewhere deep in his mind. "It's not… it's not a place like this." He gestured vaguely around them. "It's not like Pine Hollow, not like the real world. It's just—" he hesitated, his fingers twitching, like he was trying to hold onto something that was slipping away.

Dana stepped closer. "Caleb. You have to remember."

Caleb exhaled harshly, rubbing his temples. "It's like trying to remember a dream," he muttered. "I know I was there. I know there were others. But the moment I try to focus on the details, it—" He gritted his teeth. "It fades."

Dana's jaw clenched. The Watchers had taken his memory once. Maybe whatever had held him before still had its grip on him.

Caleb dragged a hand through his hair, frustration clear in his posture. "But I do remember something." His voice dropped lower. "I wasn't alone when I got out."

Dana gasped. "What?"

Caleb hesitated. "I wasn't the only one who escaped."

Dana stared at him, her mind racing. Someone else had broken out?

But then—why hadn't they seen anyone? Why hadn't anyone come looking for them?

She stepped back, shaking her head. "Then where are they?"

Caleb's expression darkened. "That's the part I can't remember."

The wind shifted.

A prickle ran up Dana's spine.

Something was watching them.

Caleb staggered.

Dana's heart jumped as Caleb's breath hitched. His posture buckled like something had just pressed down on him.

She reached for him instinctively. "Caleb—"

He flinched away.

His hands flew to his temples, his fingers digging in as if trying to hold onto something slipping through his mind.

"No," shaking his head violently. "No, no, no—"

Dana's stomach knotted. She recognized this—she had seen it before. The way Ben had struggled to remember, how the Watchers had stripped away pieces of him before he was completely erased.

And now it was happening to Caleb.

She had just watched it happen.

Caleb had been holding onto something—something big. And now? It was gone.

Erased.

Her fingers tightened on his arms. "You were just remembering something. Something important. Do you still have it?"

Caleb's brow furrowed, his confusion sharp and real. "…I don't remember remembering anything."

Dana's pulse pounded.

He wasn't lying. It was just… gone.

Like it had never been there at all.

She swallowed hard, forcing herself to keep her voice steady. "Caleb, just—just try, okay? A second ago, you were talking about others. About someone else escaping. Can you pull anything back?"

Caleb rubbed his temple, shaking his head slowly. "I don't…" His voice trailed off, his frustration deepening. "I don't remember saying that."

Dana's stomach knotted.

She had assumed breaking the cycle would be a slow process. A fight. A resistance. But this?

This was war.

And the Watchers were fighting back.

She stepped back, letting go of him. Her head spun. "They took it," she muttered. "They just—they wiped it right in front of me."

Caleb exhaled sharply, still clearly trying to grasp what she meant. "Dana, what the hell are you talking about?"

She looked up at him.

And for the first time, she felt truly alone.

Because if the Watchers could just take things back this fast—if they could erase the truth the moment it surfaced—

Then what chance did they have?

Dana staggered back, her mind racing. They weren't just watching anymore. They were taking. Actively. Aggressively.

She had never seen them move this fast.

Caleb rubbed his temple, his frustration growing. "Dana, just—talk to me. What's wrong?"

She stared at him. Wrong. Everything was wrong.

He didn't even realize it was happening.

That was the worst part.

Dana clenched her jaw, forcing herself to breathe. Panicking wouldn't help. Losing control wouldn't help.

She had to think.

The Watchers had erased Caleb's memories before. It had taken time. They had slowly pulled at him, chipped away until he was gone.

But now?

They had erased something the moment he said it.

Like they knew.

Like they had been waiting.

Dana swallowed hard. "We have to move."

Caleb exhaled sharply, still watching her with concern. "Dana—"

"We're running out of time," she snapped. "They're getting faster. They're getting worse. If we don't keep moving, you're not going to remember anything."

Caleb hesitated. She could see it—the moment of uncertainty, the moment where he wasn't sure if he trusted what she was saying.

But then—he nodded.

"Okay."

Dana turned toward the road.

They had to get somewhere safe. Somewhere Watchers couldn't reach them.

If such a place even existed anymore.

Dana's pulse pounded as she led Caleb toward the road, her mind spinning. The Watchers were changing their approach. They weren't just erasing people gradually anymore—they were striking the moment the truth surfaced.

How were they supposed to fight back against something that could undo reality itself?

Caleb stayed close, silent for once. She could feel the weight of his confusion, the tension in his movements—he didn't fully understand what had happened to him, but he could tell it was bad.

The empty road stretched ahead, lined by darkened trees. Too open. Too exposed.

Dana exhaled sharply. "We need to get off the road. We don't know how close they are."

Caleb nodded without argument. He might not remember what he had lost, but he trusted her enough to follow.

They moved fast, cutting toward the treeline. The woods loomed ahead, dense and unwelcoming, but at least they weren't standing in the open like easy targets.

Dana clutched the files tighter.

If the Watchers were this aggressive now, it meant one thing—they were afraid.

Not of Dana. Not of Caleb.

Of whatever was inside these pages.

Her mother had hidden them for a reason. Had made sure they survived.

Dana wasn't going to let the Watchers take them now.

Caleb exhaled sharply beside her, glancing toward the darkened stretch of trees ahead. "So where exactly are we going?"

Dana swallowed hard. She only had one answer.

"Somewhere they haven't erased yet."

The woods closed in around them, the branches swaying slightly in the night air. Everything felt too quiet. No wind, no rustling, no distant calls of birds or insects. Just silence.

Caleb kept pace beside her, but Dana could tell he was still unsettled—not just by what had happened, but by the gnawing feeling that something wasn't right.

She clutched the files tightly to her chest, her mind racing.

Somewhere they haven't erased yet.

What did that even mean anymore?

The Watchers had already rewritten so much. Pine Hollow wasn't the town she remembered—it was a husk, a place shaped by whatever they wanted people to believe.

If they had erased entire lives, entire families, entire histories—then where could she go that was still real?

Caleb let out a slow breath beside her. "Dana… do you even know where we're going?"

She hesitated.

Did she?

The thought made her stomach twist.

But then, deep inside her, something stirred.

Not a voice. Not a command.

Just a feeling.

A direction.

She turned slightly—not fully conscious of the decision, just following the pull inside her gut.

Caleb frowned. "Dana?"

She didn't answer.

She just kept walking.

Because something inside her knew where to go.

Even if she didn't understand why.

Dana moved without thinking, her feet finding an unmarked path through the trees.

The pull inside her wasn't logical. It wasn't something she could explain.

But it was there.

And it was leading her somewhere real.

Caleb hesitated but didn't stop her. "Dana—where are we going?"

"I don't know," she admitted. But she didn't slow down.

Caleb muttered something under his breath but followed. The woods thickened around them, the air heavy, dense with something she couldn't name.

Dana's grip tightened on the files. The Watchers couldn't erase everything. They could rewrite, distort, erase memories, people, places—

But not this.

Not wherever she was going.

The ground sloped downward, the trees pressing closer. The feeling inside her chest grew stronger, more insistent.

Then, ahead—a break in the trees.

Dana froze.

Caleb stopped beside her. "What is it?"

She swallowed hard. The sight before her didn't make sense.

A house.

Not abandoned. Not ruined.

A house that looked untouched by time.

Caleb exhaled. "You know this place?"

Dana's fingers trembled around the files.

"…I think I do."

She took a step forward.

The house was waiting.

Dana stepped closer, her breath shallow.

The house stood perfectly still, untouched by the years, untouched by the Watchers.

That shouldn't be possible.

Caleb moved beside her, his eyes scanning the exterior. "What is this place?"

Dana didn't answer immediately.

Because the moment she saw it, she knew.

Not because she recognized it. Not exactly.

But because the same feeling that had guided her here—the pull, the certainty—was humming inside her chest.

This place mattered.

This place was real.

She swallowed hard and stepped forward. The porch creaked beneath her boots, but the house itself felt sturdy. Not like something abandoned, but like something preserved.

Caleb hesitated. "Dana, are we just gonna walk into some stranger's house?"

Dana reached for the door handle. It turned easily.

Unlocked.

She pushed the door open.

Inside—nothing was covered in dust. No sheets thrown over furniture. No broken windows, no decay.

It was lived in.

Like whoever had been here had only just left.

Caleb exhaled sharply behind her. "What the hell…"

Dana stepped inside.

And then—she saw the photograph.

Sitting on a small table by the entrance, waiting for her.

She walked toward it, slowly, carefully, her fingers hovering just over the frame.

The moment she saw the faces inside, her breath caught.

Her mother.

And Miriam.

Standing together, smiling.

And beneath it, scrawled in her mother's handwriting—

"This is where it begins."

Dana's fingers trembled as she picked up the photograph.

Her mother's handwriting.

Her mother's words.

This is where it begins.

Her throat tightened. This wasn't just another relic of the past—this was intentional. Placed here, waiting for her.

Caleb stepped closer, peering over her shoulder. He exhaled sharply. "That's your mom."

Dana nodded, barely breathing.

He pointed to the other woman in the photo. Miriam.

"Guess that means she's been around longer than I thought."

Dana ignored the comment. She was too focused on the photo—on the look in her mother's eyes.

She wasn't just smiling.

She looked certain.

Like she had known something no one else did.

Dana swallowed hard and turned the frame over. Something was taped to the back.

A key.

She plucked it off carefully, feeling the cool metal press into her palm.

Caleb frowned. "What's that for?"

Dana looked up, scanning the house.

And then—her eyes landed on the hallway.

A door at the very end.

Closed.

Waiting.

Her mother had left her something.

And Dana was about to find out what.

Dana's pulse hammered as she clutched the key.

The door at the end of the hallway stood perfectly still.

Waiting.

Caleb shifted beside her. "Dana." His voice was quiet, edged with caution.

She didn't answer.

She just started walking.

The wooden floor was solid beneath her steps. Not warped with age, not creaking under weight. This house had not been abandoned.

Everything about it felt preserved. Intact. Untouched by the erasures.

She stopped in front of the door. The key fit the lock perfectly.

A soft click.

The door swung inward.

And inside—her breath caught.

A study.

A desk pushed against the far wall. Shelves lined with books, neat stacks of papers, an old lamp still poised over an open notebook.

It wasn't covered in dust.

It wasn't forgotten.

It looked like someone had been here recently.

Like her mother had just stepped out.

Caleb exhaled behind her. "What the hell is this place?"

Dana tightened her grip on the files from the library, her fingers pressing into the worn pages.

Because for the first time since she had stolen them—they didn't feel like the most important thing in her hands anymore.

Her gaze locked onto something else.

A single stack of papers sitting at the center of the desk.

Her mother's handwriting.

Waiting for her.

Dana hesitated, her fingers hovering over the stack of papers.

She still had the files from the library clutched tightly in her arms. Pages filled with erased names, missing people, a history the Watchers had tried to bury.

And now—her mother's notes.

The air inside the study felt thicker now, like something was waiting to be found.

Slowly, carefully, Dana set the library files down on the desk, her eyes scanning both stacks of documents. Something about this felt deliberate.

Like her mother had known.

Caleb stood beside her, silent for once. Watching.

Dana exhaled and flipped open the first page of her mother's notes.

The handwriting was hurried, but precise. Underlined. Dated. Documented.

And the first thing she saw was a name she already knew.

Morgan Reece.

Caleb leaned over, frowning. "That's—"

"Morgan," Dana whispered. "She's in the library files."

She grabbed one of the pages she had stolen, scanning through the notes—her pulse spiked.

Her mother had been keeping her own records.

She hadn't just known about the missing people. She had been tracking them.

And then—at the bottom of the page, her mother's words, scribbled in ink.

"The Watchers don't erase everyone the same way. Some are lost completely. Others... are held."

Dana's hands shook.

Her mother had been searching for them.

For the ones the Watchers kept.

The same ones Caleb had just started to remember.

And then—a noise.

Soft. Almost imperceptible.

But enough to tell Dana they weren't alone in the house anymore.

Dana's blood ran cold.

The house had been silent since they stepped inside.

Still. Waiting.

But now—

Something had changed.

Caleb tensed beside her. He had heard it too.

A sound.

Soft. Faint. A shift in the air, a creak in the floorboards.

Dana whipped her head toward the doorway, her pulse hammering. The hallway beyond was dark, the open door leading into an empty house.

Nothing there.

But she knew better.

She glanced back at the desk—at the files, her mother's notes. The answers they had been chasing, the proof that everything they feared was true.

The Watchers don't erase everyone the same way.

Her mother had written that. She had known.

Caleb moved slowly, his hand hovering near his side, like instinct was telling him to reach for a weapon—except he didn't have one.

Dana exhaled carefully, forcing her voice low. "We're not alone."

Caleb's jaw tightened. "I know."

Another noise.

This time, closer.

Dana snatched the files off the desk, shoving them into her bag without thinking. Whatever was in this house with them—

It didn't want them reading this.

The air grew heavier.

A whisper—not words, just the feeling of something pressing against the edges of her mind.

Caleb spoke softly. "Dana—"

The lights flickered.

The door slammed shut.

Dana took a sharp breath.

The air inside the study thickened, pressing against her skin like a weight. The lights flickered again, stuttering between dim and total darkness.

Caleb swore under his breath, stepping back instinctively. "That's not the wind, is it?"

Dana didn't answer.

She was already moving, shoving her mother's notes into her bag with the stolen files. She didn't know how much time they had, but she wasn't leaving anything behind.

Caleb's breathing turned sharp. He was staring at the door now, his body tense. "There's something on the other side."

Dana froze.

Then she heard it too.

A slow, deliberate scrape.

Not like footsteps.

Not like something moving toward them.

Like something dragging itself along the floor.

Caleb's fingers twitched at his sides. He had no weapon. No gun, no knife, nothing but his hands.

And Dana—she had nothing either.

Just the files.

Just the truth.

And the Watchers didn't want her to have either.

Another scrape. Closer this time.

Caleb inhaled sharply. "What do we do?"

Dana clenched her jaw.

They had to get out.

But before she could answer—

The light went out completely.

Darkness swallowed the room.

Not dim light. Not shadows. Total, suffocating blackness.

Dana's breath came fast and sharp. She couldn't see Caleb, couldn't see the door, couldn't see anything.

The air felt thicker now, pressing against her skin. Something was here.

Caleb moved beside her, the shift in the floorboards the only indication he was still there. "Dana—"

Then, from the other side of the door—

The whispering returned.

Not loud. Soft. Crawling.

A voice almost familiar.

Caleb tensed. "Dana—"

The whisper cut through the dark.

"You shouldn't have come here."

Dana's stomach plummeted.

She knew that voice.

It was her mother's.

But it wasn't real.

It couldn't be real.

Her throat tightened. "You're not her."

Silence.

Then—something scratched against the door.

Slow. Purposeful.

The whispering grew distorted, warping into something deeper, something stretched and wrong.

Caleb's breathing sharpened. He wasn't seeing what she was, but he could feel it.

Dana swallowed hard. They had to get out.

She reached blindly in the dark, fingers brushing against the surface of the desk, the edges of the books, searching.

Then—the door handle rattled.

Something was trying to get in.

Caleb moved fast, grabbing Dana's arm,pulling her back. "We need to—"

The door burst open.

And the whispering poured inside.

The whispering rushed into the room like a wave, thick and suffocating, curling around Dana's ears.

Not just her mother's voice now. Others. Stacked. Layered. Crawling over each other.

Caleb pulled her back sharply, his breath ragged. "Dana, MOVE."

She didn't hesitate.

They bolted.

Dana ducked low, dragging Caleb with her as they pushed past the door. The air in the hallway felt wrong—denser, colder, warped. **But they couldn't stop.**

Something moved behind them. Not footsteps. Something shifting, dragging.

The whispering chased them.

Caleb cursed under his breath, throwing a glance over his shoulder. "Don't look back—just GO."

Dana's grip tightened on her bag, her lungs burning as they sprinted toward the front door.

They weren't alone in the house.

And whatever was here—it wasn't letting them leave easily.

Caleb reached the door first, yanking at the handle.

Locked.

"It was open before—"

A creak above them.

Dana froze.

Caleb's gaze snapped upward.

Something was on the ceiling.

Watching.

Waiting.

And then—

It dropped.

The figure dropped from the ceiling with unnerving grace, its body long, spindly, and impossibly twisted as it landed between them and the door.

Dana stumbled backward, her breath catching in her throat. She couldn't see its face—just the vague, shifting outline that was almost human but wrong.

It was the way it moved—too fast, too fluid, like it wasn't bound by the same rules as them.

Caleb stepped in front of her, his voice low but urgent. "Stay behind me. Don't—"

But before he could finish, the figure lunged toward him.

He dove to the side, narrowly avoiding its reach, the air around them tensing like it was holding its breath.

Dana's mind raced. The door was locked. The window wasn't an option. They had nowhere to go.

She grabbed Caleb's arm. "We need to fight back. Now!"

The figure's head tilted, its eyes flashing for a moment—empty, hollow, like it wasn't looking at them, but through them.

The whispering returned—this time, it was louder, closer, like the walls themselves were humming with it.

Caleb gritted his teeth, fists clenched, his back pressed against the wall. He took a deep breath, his eyes flashing toward Dana. "Do you have anything?"

Dana shook her head, feeling the weight of her bag pull against her shoulder.

There was nothing in it but papers, files.

No weapons. No escape.

And the thing in front of them wasn't backing down.

With a sudden shift, the creature lunged forward again, and this time, Dana didn't wait for Caleb to act. She grabbed the first thing she could—a lamp from the desk—and swung it as hard as she could.

The lamp connected with the creature with a sickening crack.

It shrieked, but the sound wasn't human. It ripped through her skull, a noise that made her stomach churn.

But the thing didn't falter.

It just shuddered, its body ripping apart at the edges, like it was warping into something even worse.

Dana's chest tightened. "Caleb, we need to MOVE."

He didn't argue.

They ran—pushing through the hallway toward the back door, the creature's screeching still ringing in their ears.

Dana and Caleb ran, their feet pounding against the wooden floors, the sound of the creature's screeching following them like an echo in their minds. The air around them felt thick, the weight of whatever force had been unleashed pressing down on their shoulders.

The back door was only a few feet away, but Dana's pulse was hammering so hard she could barely think. Her mind raced, searching for any way out.

Behind them, the creature's shrill cry echoed, distorted by its unnatural shape, as though the sound didn't belong in the same space. Closer now.

Caleb's voice was tight, his breath ragged. "We can't outrun it!"

Dana didn't look back, but she could feel it—the thing right behind them, its presence hanging in the air like a dark storm cloud.

With one last desperate motion, Dana reached for the back door's handle. Unlocked.

She yanked it open, the cool night air flooding in like a rush of fresh oxygen.

They both stumbled outside, barely clear of the threshold, when the door slammed shut behind them with a force that made the entire house shudder.

Caleb turned, his chest heaving, but Dana couldn't stop. They had to keep moving.

She pulled him forward into the darkness, the familiar layout of the yard now distorted by the terror she felt. The house was behind them, but that didn't matter. They weren't safe yet.

She felt the pull again—the strange sensation deep in her gut that told her they had to go toward the trees.

Caleb glanced over at her, his eyes wide with confusion. "Dana—what are you doing? We don't have time—"

"We do," she snapped. "We're not staying out in the open."

He hesitated but followed.

Dana pushed through the underbrush, her breath sharp in the still night air. Behind them, she could feel the creature's presence linger, but it wasn't chasing them. It was watching—waiting for the right moment to strike again.

She could feel its eyes on her.

But the trees felt like a temporary sanctuary. The thick canopy above them blocked out the sky, shrouding them in shadow. She couldn't hear the creature anymore, but the whispering had shifted, and it still carried a warning in the back of her mind.

They slowed, their breaths coming faster now, and Dana stopped, her eyes scanning the area.

Caleb was about to speak when a low, guttural growl cut through the air—a sound that wasn't from the creature they had left behind.

Her heart skipped.

This wasn't over.

The low, guttural growl sent a jolt of fear through Dana. It was deep—unnatural, like it came from somewhere far below the earth.

She and Caleb froze in place. The creature, whatever it was, had stopped chasing them—but the sense of dread didn't leave. It was still there, hanging in the air, pressing in from all sides.

Caleb's voice was a low whisper. "What the hell was that?"

Dana's heart was racing, but she couldn't answer right away. She was too focused on the sound—the way it lingered in the stillness of the woods.

She squinted into the darkness ahead. The trees were thick, the shadows too deep to make out anything beyond a few feet, but she could feel it watching.

The growl came again, this time much closer. It was circling them.

Caleb stiffened. "We need to move."

Dana nodded, but as they started to move forward, something shifted in the air—like the ground had pulled away from under them, creating an invisible pressure that forced their feet to drag.

Dana reached out instinctively, grabbing Caleb's arm. "Wait—did you feel that?"

He nodded, his eyes wide. "Something's… wrong. We're not moving forward. We're not getting away from it."

It wasn't just the sound anymore—it was the way the air felt wrong, like it was bending and twisting around them. The trees seemed to loom closer, pressing in like they were closing in.

And then—another growl.

Not from the woods. Not from the creature.

From the ground itself.

The earth under their feet shifted again, and Dana's stomach dropped. It was like the world was rearranging—changing shape—as if it didn't want them to escape.

Caleb looked around frantically. "We're trapped."

Dana gripped his arm tighter. "No—we're not. We have to—"

But before she could finish, a shadow shifted ahead.

And then—it was there.

The creature.

It was crawling out of the ground. Its long, twisted limbs seemed to burst from the earth like roots, its eyes glowing with that eerie, unnatural light.

Caleb didn't hesitate. He pulled Dana back, but it was too late. The creature's form was almost solid now, its body twitching, like it was adjusting itself to the real world.

They had nowhere to run.

Dana's heart raced as she grabbed the bag at her side, pulling out the files again—just in case. She had to keep moving, keep thinking. She wasn't going to let this thing take them without a fight.

Caleb's grip tightened on her arm. "Dana—"

But he didn't finish.

The creature lunged.

The creature lunged forward, its twisted limbs snapping through the air toward them, its mouth opening to reveal rows of teeth that weren't just for show.

Dana's breath caught in her throat, her heart hammering in her chest. She barely had time to react before Caleb shoved her behind him, his body blocking the creature's path.

"Caleb!" Dana shouted, her hand reaching for him, but he was already moving, throwing his weight into the creature. The impact knocked them both backward.

Dana scrambled to her feet, her mind racing. She couldn't let this happen. They had to break free. The creature wasn't just a beast—it was connected to the cycle. Its very existence was designed to ensure they never left.

The ground shuddered beneath her feet as the creature's limbs shot out, wrapping around Caleb's torso like a vine. He grunted, struggling to break free, but the thing's grip was unrelenting. It was dragging him toward it, its mouth widening.

Dana didn't hesitate.

With a scream, she ran forward, her hand flying into her bag for the files, but it wasn't the files she pulled out this time.

It was the key.

Without thinking, she jammed it into the creature's body, slamming it in with all her strength. The creature's body twitched, its grip loosening on Caleb as it let out a low wail—more in surprise than in pain.

Dana didn't give it a second thought. She pulled Caleb away, yanking him back to his feet, their bodies stumbling together.

"We need to get out," Dana panted, shoving the key back into her bag.

Caleb was breathing heavily, but his eyes were clearer now. "What the hell was that?"

"I don't know," Dana whispered, "but I think the key… it did something."

They didn't stop to look back. The creature was twitching, its form still shifting and distorting, but it wasn't pursuing them anymore. It was as though the key had unsettled it, thrown it off balance in some way.

Dana's hand gripped Caleb's as they stumbled back toward the trees. The forest was still dark, but the air around them felt less oppressive now—for a moment, it was like the shadows had loosened their grip.

They kept moving, pushing through the thick underbrush, their breaths ragged, not speaking until they were sure they were far enough away to finally stop.

Caleb wiped his brow. "What the hell is going on, Dana? First the town, then Miriam, now this?"

Dana exhaled sharply, her mind spinning. "I don't know. But I think we're getting closer to the truth. And I don't think the Watchers want us to find it."

Caleb didn't say anything right away, but he looked at her, eyes heavy with unspoken understanding.

"We'll figure this out," he said, his voice rough but steady.

Dana nodded, but inside she felt the weight of the world pressing against her chest. They weren't just fighting for their survival. They were fighting against something that had been controlling this town—this reality—for far too long.

And whatever it was, it was not going to let them win easily.

They stumbled through the forest, the weight of what had just happened pressing down on them. The air felt still, too still, as if the entire world was holding its breath, waiting for the next move.

Dana kept her focus ahead, pushing through the underbrush, but her mind was racing. The key, the creature, and now the realization that they were being watched—trapped in a cycle they didn't fully understand.

Caleb kept pace beside her, his steps slow but determined. He didn't say anything more about the creature or the house. They both knew it was a temporary victory, but it didn't feel like they were out of danger yet.

And then—the pull came again.

That quiet tug deep in her gut, urging her forward. It wasn't just the way the trees were positioned or the feel of the ground beneath her feet. It was like something beyond the physical was calling her.

She stopped, her hand still gripping Caleb's arm. "It's this way," she murmured, more to herself than to him.

Caleb looked at her, confusion flashing in his eyes. "What?"

Dana didn't answer immediately. She turned, pushing through the thickening forest, drawn toward something she couldn't explain. The pull was stronger now—familiar, insistent.

Caleb followed, though his confusion deepened. "You feel that too, don't you?"

Dana nodded, her heart pounding. She did feel it. It was like an invisible thread, leading her forward. She couldn't explain it, but she knew it was the right direction.

And when she looked up, the trees opened up ahead, revealing a clearing she didn't remember from before.

In the center of it, something gleamed.

A stone.

Not just any stone—this one was carved, like a marker, a signpost for something deeper. Something important.

Caleb looked at it, then back at her. "What the hell is that?"

Dana's fingers trembled as she stepped forward. She reached out for the stone, her breath held tight in her chest. The pull was stronger here—it wasn't just calling her, it was binding her.

As her fingers brushed against the surface, the air shifted—and for a moment, she was somewhere else.

Flashes of images—her mother's face, Miriam, the erased people—rushed through her mind, but it wasn't just memories. It was knowledge. The kind of knowledge that felt dangerous to hold.

She gasped, pulling her hand back.

Caleb looked at her in alarm. "Dana, what is it?"

Dana's breath was shallow. She didn't have the answers—but she was closer. She could feel it.

She turned back to the stone, her voice barely a whisper. "It's a marker. This is where they've been hiding everything."

Caleb's voice broke through her thoughts. "And the key?"

Dana didn't answer right away. The key had done something to the creature, thrown it off balance—but it was clear now that it was just a piece of the puzzle.

"Maybe it's part of the way out," she said, her voice low. "But I think we need to go deeper. There's more."

Before Caleb could respond, the wind picked up—a sudden gust that cut through the clearing, sending a chill down Dana's spine. She felt the shift in the air, that same feeling of something closing in, like they weren't alone.

Something was watching them.

The wind howled, the trees swaying violently, as though the very forest was trying to push them away.

Dana's breath quickened as she felt it—the unseen presence, the shift in the atmosphere. Something was closing in, just beyond the edge of her perception.

Caleb stiffened beside her, his eyes scanning the darkness that surrounded them. "Dana... what the hell is happening?"

She didn't have an answer. The feeling was suffocating, like the air itself was thickening, pressing them inward, toward the stone.

And then—a sound.

Soft at first, almost imperceptible.

A whisper.

The same voice they had heard before—the creature, or whatever force was controlling it.

This time, though, the voice was clearer.

"You cannot escape."

The air around them rippled, as if the words had a physical weight, forcing the world to warp in response. The ground beneath their feet shifted, the earth buckling under an unseen pressure.

Caleb reached out, grabbing Dana's arm. "We need to move. NOW."

But Dana couldn't move—she was rooted in place, her fingers still trembling from the contact with the stone. Something inside her had clicked. It wasn't just the pull anymore—there was knowledge here. A key to understanding what had been erased, what had been hidden from them.

Her eyes narrowed, focusing on the stone again, and she could see it more clearly now—carved symbols, ancient markings that had been etched into the surface, glowing faintly.

The whispering voice grew louder, more insistent.

"You are part of the cycle. You cannot break free."

Dana's heart raced, and with every beat, the pull grew stronger. The cycle—this was what the Watchers had built, the endless rewriting, the erasure of everything that threatened their control. She could feel the truth forming in her mind, pieces clicking into place.

And then—a flash.

A vision.

Her mother.

Standing at the same stone, touching it, her face filled with determination, a faint smile at the edge of her lips.

"This is where it begins."

Dana's hand shot up, her fingers brushing the surface of the stone once more, and this time—the symbols flared.

The air around them exploded with energy, a shockwave rippling outward, knocking them both back. Dana slammed into the ground, her breath knocked out of her.

Caleb shouted, reaching for her, but Dana could barely hear him over the deafening sound that followed—the crackling energy, the sensation of something breaking open in the world around them.

And then—silence.

Dana opened her eyes, her body aching from the fall, and she realized—the stone was gone.

The clearing was empty.

No stone.

No presence.

Just the night air.

She sat up slowly, breathing heavily. What had just happened?

Caleb helped her to her feet, his face a mix of confusion and fear. "What the hell was that?"

Dana shook her head, still trying to process. "I don't know. But I think we've just set something in motion."

The forest was still, the air no longer thick with pressure. But Dana could feel it—the tension in the air was still there, lurking just beyond her reach.

It wasn't over.

It had only just begun.

Dana stood slowly, her legs trembling as she tried to ground herself in the stillness of the clearing. The air was thick with something—uncertainty, as if the world itself was holding its breath. She could feel the absence of the stone, the absence of whatever power had been holding them.

Caleb took a cautious step forward, his eyes scanning the empty space where the stone had been. "What the hell just happened? That felt like—like something was ripped open."

Dana nodded, her gaze still fixed on the spot. "It did. I think we…" She swallowed hard, trying to make sense of the sudden shift. "I think we broke something. Something that was keeping this place under control."

Caleb frowned, glancing around. "Is it gone? The thing we were running from?"

Dana didn't answer immediately. She could still feel it—the pull—but it wasn't the same. It wasn't watching them anymore. It was like the presence had shifted, as though the cycle had been broken open, leaving them in a state of limbo.

She turned to face him. "I don't think the creature's gone, but it's not chasing us anymore."

Caleb raised an eyebrow. "What the hell does that mean?"

Dana opened her mouth to respond, but before she could speak, a low rumble shook the ground beneath them. It wasn't loud—not at first—but it was enough to send a shiver down her spine. The forest shifted again, and the trees around them seemed to bend inward, as if closing in on them.

Caleb took a step back. "Dana…"

Dana's heartbeat sped up, her senses on high alert. The whispering was gone, but now—this. Something was coming. Something new.

Then, out of the corner of her eye, she saw it. A figure, standing still at the edge of the clearing.

Not a person.

Not a thing she recognized.

It was dark, its shape blurred, like it was flickering in and out of existence.

Dana felt her stomach tighten, her body going rigid with the knowledge that this was something far worse than what they had just faced.

Caleb reached for her arm, pulling her back. "We need to move—NOW."

But Dana didn't move.

She couldn't move.

The figure stepped forward, closer—its form solidifying as it did.

And then it spoke.

"You shouldn't have broken it."

The voice was like a whisper on the wind, but there was something forceful about it, something that felt like it was reaching directly into her mind.

Dana's legs shook, her entire body fighting the instinct to run. "Who are you?" she demanded, her voice shaky but defiant.

The figure tilted its head, as if considering her question.

And then—it smiled.

But the smile wasn't human. It was too wide, too sharp.

"I am the consequence."

Dana and Caleb stood frozen in the clearing, their breath quick and shallow, as the consequence creature towered before them. Its dark form still flickering, almost like it was materializing and disintegrating at the same time. Its face—or what passed for a face—was too sharp, too wide, stretching unnaturally as it tilted its head to study them.

The weight of its words hung heavily in the air. "You shouldn't have broken it."

Dana's pulse pounded in her ears. The weight of the creature's presence pressed down on her chest, like an invisible force trying to crush her. She swallowed hard, trying to steady herself.

"What do you want from us?" she demanded, her voice unsteady but fierce.

The creature didn't respond right away, just stared at her, its eyes black pits that seemed to absorb the light around them. For a moment, Dana felt like the entire world was being drawn into those dark depths. It was as though the creature wasn't just a thing in front of them, but the embodiment of every force that had been trying to keep them trapped.

Caleb stepped forward, his voice cutting through the oppressive silence. "You can't stop us. We're not done yet."

The creature's smile stretched wider, its body warping and twisting. "You can't even see the edges of this world, let alone the truth."

Dana's breath caught. The cycle, the erased, the truth about the town—everything they had been chasing, everything they had been threatened by—it was more than just them.

The creature's voice was low now, almost like a hum. "The truth will never be yours."

Dana's mind raced. The key—the stone—had connected her to something deeper, something bigger. But the creature, whatever it was, was warning them that they were in too deep now, that there were consequences for even trying to understand it.

Caleb clenched his fists, ready to fight, but Dana held out a hand. She could feel the pull again—the same one that had led her to the stone, to the realization that something was wrong. The same one that had kept her fighting even when the weight of the world felt like it was too much to bear.

She turned to Caleb, her eyes steady. "We're not backing down."

Caleb looked at her, confusion and determination mixing in his gaze. "Then what are we supposed to do now?"

The creature's twisted form began to shimmer, its body flickering in and out of focus as it hovered closer, as if it were about to strike.

Dana felt a sudden surge of power—something deep within her, something she hadn't fully understood until now. The key, the stone, her mother's handwriting—it all started to click.

"We keep moving forward," Dana said, her voice steady despite the weight of the situation. "We find out what's really happening here. And we break it. Whatever it takes."

The creature's expression twisted, its smile faltering for just a moment. "You're too late."

But before it could act, the air shifted again—something unexpected—and the creature recoiled. It seemed to shrink back into the shadows, its form warping as if it could no longer fully maintain its physical presence.

Dana didn't hesitate. "Now, Caleb!"

They ran.

Chapter 11

Dana's breath came in ragged gasps as she and Caleb pushed through the forest, their feet barely skimming over the underbrush. The air around them seemed to grow heavier, thick with something unnatural. They were still running from the Consequence Creature, the sound of its twisted limbs scraping over the forest floor just behind them.

Caleb glanced back, his face pale with fear. "It's gaining on us!"

Dana didn't need to look back to know. The creature was relentless, its inhuman shrieks cutting through the trees, getting closer with every passing second. Its dark, flickering form was shadowing their every move, its limbs snapping through the air with an eerie, impossible speed.

But Dana didn't stop. She couldn't.

"Keep going!" she shouted to Caleb, pulling him forward, her hand gripping his arm tightly. The pull—the feeling she'd had since the beginning of this journey—was growing stronger.

It wasn't just the fear driving her now. Something else was at play. She could feel it, like a compass pulling her in the right direction, urging her to keep moving forward. It was as if the ground beneath her feet was guiding her, the forest itself whispering to her, telling her where to go.

Dana didn't know how she knew it—she just did.

She felt Miriam's presence, or at least, the energy she believed was coming from Miriam, wherever she was. It was like a silent hand, gently but firmly pushing her toward the answers she needed. She wasn't sure how it was happening, but the closer they got to the center of the woods, the more she felt like she was being guided.

Caleb's voice broke through her thoughts. "What's happening, Dana? Where are we going?"

Dana didn't answer at first. Her focus was entirely on the invisible force leading her, on the energy that was pulling her toward the unknown. It was as if something far beyond her control was steering her toward the stone, toward the place where everything would finally break free.

She felt it—the ground beneath her feet felt different now. It wasn't just earth; it was something alive, something connected to everything. She could feel the weight of what was ahead, the closeness of their destination.

Caleb looked around, confusion growing in his eyes. "Dana, what are you—"

"I don't know how I know," she said breathlessly, "but I know this is where we're supposed to be."

She didn't stop running, didn't look back, even as the creature's screeching became deafening behind them. They were nearly there—she could feel it. The stone. The key to breaking everything.

Caleb was silent now, but he followed, trusting her despite the confusion in his mind. They had no choice but to keep going.

And then, through the trees—they saw it.

The clearing opened up before them, and Dana skidded to a halt. In front of her, partially hidden by the trees, was a stone structure, its surface marked with symbols that she'd seen before—in the files, in her mother's notes.

She stepped forward, her heart pounding as if she were walking into the final battle. The energy here was overwhelming. She could feel Miriam—or at least, the energy that had been guiding her—was now surrounding the stone, pulling her toward it.

"This is it," Dana whispered, looking at Caleb. "This is where it ends."

Caleb was about to respond when the shadows in the woods moved.

Dana's stomach dropped. She felt it first—the familiar presence of the Consequence Creature closing in. The pull was stronger than ever, but this time, it wasn't just leading them toward the stone—it was leading them toward the final confrontation.

The creature emerged from the trees with terrifying speed, its twisted limbs and dark shape charging toward them. The air around them grew thick with pressure, the ground shuddering underfoot.

Dana grabbed Caleb's arm. "Move—now!"

They broke into a sprint, but the creature was right behind them. It was a beast of nightmare, closing the gap with every step. Dana could feel the rush of air as its twisted limbs swiped through the trees, its shrill screech echoing through the forest.

Her breath was quick, her body aching, but the pull she felt was stronger than ever, guiding her toward something she couldn't yet explain. She didn't dare look back, but her heart pounded with the knowledge that if they didn't get to the clearing soon, they might not make it.

They finally burst into the clearing, and Dana's eyes went wide. The stone stood before them—marked with symbols she recognized, the key to breaking the cycle. But as her feet touched the ground, she felt it—Miriam's presence, surrounding her, filling the air with a familiar, protective energy.

She stopped dead in her tracks, turning instinctively toward the edge of the forest, where something was emerging from the shadows.

The Consequence Creature stepped into the clearing, its long, gnarled limbs stretching toward them, its mouth widening in a terrible, soundless snarl. It moved slowly, but each step seemed to shake the earth beneath them.

Dana's heart skipped. But then, just as the creature's gaze locked onto them, Hollow materialized in front of it—a shadow stepping into being, his form taking shape from the darkness itself. He stood tall, his presence so overpowering that even the creature faltered for a moment.

The two beings faced each other, a tense silence hanging in the air as they regarded one another. The Consequence Creature seemed to hesitate, its glowing eyes flickering between Hollow and Dana. The air hummed with a tension neither of them could escape.

After a long, almost unnatural pause, the creature finally turned its attention back to Dana and Caleb. But Hollow did not move.

Instead, Hollow's focus shifted—his gaze slowly turning toward Dana and Caleb. The air around them seemed to tighten as Hollow's eyes locked on Dana. His presence grew colder, more forceful.

Without warning, Hollow twitched—a small, almost imperceptible movement—but it was enough.

Caleb collapsed to the ground, his body unable to resist the force. His eyes fluttered, but he was not fully unconscious—his expression remained blank, his body limp.

Dana stood still as the power of the Hollow's presence tried to claim her. She felt the tug of his force, but it didn't touch her.

She was unaffected, rooted to the spot by the resonance of her connection to the world around her—and, perhaps, something greater that had been awakening inside her.

Hollow's eyes narrowed. He wasn't pleased. He stepped forward, his feet barely touching the ground as he approached Dana.

Dana's breath caught, and for a moment, it seemed like everything might end here.

But as Hollow came closer, Miriam—her presence becoming palpable, unmistakable—moved past Dana without a word, walking directly toward Hollow.

It was as if the world shifted around them, the weight of the moment drawing everything in as Miriam and Hollow faced each other, the final showdown about to unfold.

Miriam stood tall, her presence commanding the air around her. The light that enveloped her seemed to pulse with each breath she took, like the very essence of the forest was shifting in response to her. Hollow's dark form hovered in front of her, his features hard and unmoving, but his eyes flickered with something unnatural—a glare that sent a shiver down Dana's spine.

Dana stood frozen, watching the exchange unfold. Miriam was more than she had ever known, and yet she felt incredibly small at that moment, the weight of what was happening pressing down on her chest. The air was thick with suspense, the ground beneath them trembling ever so slightly as if the world itself was holding its breath.

Hollow's gaze never left Miriam as he stepped forward, his movements slow, deliberate. The consequence creature, though still looming nearby, seemed to shrink back as if even it recognized the weight of the conflict about to unfold. Hollow's voice was low, almost a growl as he spoke, but it carried an intensity that filled the clearing. "You should not have interfered."

Miriam's response was calm, almost serene, but it carried a power that made the air hum. "It is too late for that." She stepped closer to Hollow, and at that moment, Dana felt the energy around them shift like the very atmosphere was thickening with every step Miriam took.

Suddenly, Miriam's form seemed to blur—her outline flickered, almost as if she were too bright, too powerful to remain in her human shape. The light that had surrounded her now intensified, and her body seemed to stretch, becoming larger, more transcendent, like she was no longer bound to any earthly form.

Her eyes burned with a fierce glow, the iris shifting from a soft, warm hue to a piercing light that was almost blinding. It wasn't just light that emanated from her; it felt like raw power, the kind that was older than time itself. The air crackled around her as the energy grew, and the earth beneath their feet seemed to hum, vibrating in resonance with her transformation.

Miriam's figure became less human and more like a manifestation of energy—ethereal and radiant but also terrifying in its intensity. Her hands spread wide, and the very ground seemed to pulse with each movement. The stone beneath her feet shifted, glowing in response to her power, as if acknowledging her dominance over this moment.

Her true form was no longer the frail, elderly woman Dana had known. She had become something far beyond—a being that radiated power in its purest form, the kind of energy that could reshape reality itself. She was almost translucent as if she were both here and not, a being forged from the fabric of the very universe itself, transcending space and time.

Hollow's eyes narrowed, but he didn't move. The air was thick with the tension of their standoff, the ground beneath their feet vibrating as Miriam's true form took full shape. She towered over them, not with physical height, but with an energy that seemed to reach into the very fabric of the world, and for a moment, the earth bowed to her.

The Consequence Creature, still looming in the background, shifted uneasily at the sight of her. It made a low, guttural sound, almost as though it could feel the shift in the very air around them—its dark form flickered, but its resolve remained. It stepped forward, its limbs stretching as it prepared to act, to strike again.

Without a word, Miriam raised one hand. The creature's movements froze mid-step. It stilled as if caught in an unseen web. Miriam's hand glowed, not with light, but with a force so pure and absolute that the creature couldn't move, couldn't breathe. It was as though time itself halted in her presence.

She didn't need to speak; her will alone was enough. The creature let out a final, desperate hiss, but in an instant, it crumbled, its form unraveling like a shadow being erased by the sun's first light. It collapsed into nothingness—effortlessly dispelled, its existence snuffed out with barely a flicker of energy from Miriam.

Dana, stunned, watched as the Consequence Creature simply ceased to exist, its form dissolving into the air with a whisper. The clearing, once tense with fear, now felt quiet, even serene, as if the threat had never been there at all.

Miriam turned her gaze back to Hollow, her eyes still burning bright with that unfathomable power. She didn't need to say anything more—the message was clear.

The clearing fell silent after the Consequence Creature's final wail, its form dissolving into nothingness at Miriam's command. The air around them had shifted—what was once tense with dread now felt almost peaceful, as though the earth itself had exhaled in relief. The battle had only just begun, but one threat had been neutralized effortlessly, leaving Hollow standing alone.

Dana's heart still hammered in her chest, her breath quick and shallow. She stood frozen, watching Miriam, her true form radiating more power than she had ever imagined. There was a stillness to her now—her energy humming through the air like a cosmic force that could reshape reality itself. Hollow, despite his dark presence, remained unmoving.

Miriam's eyes never left him. "You've been a part of this, Hollow," she said, her voice low, not with anger, but with something older. "You helped build it."

Hollow's form flickered, a ripple passing through his body as if his very existence were being tested. His response came slowly, with deliberate calmness. "You may have stopped me for now, but this is only the beginning. You think you know what you're doing? Do you understand what breaking the cycle will cause?" His voice held an edge, the underlying threat unmistakable.

Miriam's gaze hardened. "Yes. And I'll do the same to her."

For the briefest moment, Dana thought she saw a shift in Hollow's expression—was it fear? His presence seemed to grow darker, like the shadows themselves were reacting to his frustration, but he did not retreat. Miriam's power, unchallenged as it was, did not faze him. His cold determination burned even brighter in the face of her unrelenting force.

Dana felt the air tighten around her as Hollow's presence shifted, though his form remained largely unchanged. But Miriam wasn't finished. Her eyes glowed brighter, casting shadows deeper as she stepped forward, her movements deliberate and graceful.

"You don't get to decide anymore," she said. The words were simple, but there was a finality in them as if she were cutting through a web of lies, tearing it down piece by piece.

Before Miriam could react, Hollow's shadowy figure reached and grasped her throat. Hollow resisted the intense burn from her radiating light as he tightened his grip.

"Mother must not be..." he said as his shadow-covered arm burned.

In an instant, Miriam raised her hand once more, this time not in aggression but in utter command. The energy around her rippled again, the very ground beneath them responding to her will. Hollow flinched. His arm shot back as he stumbled. The clearing hummed, a steady vibration coursing through the earth, through the trees. The world seemed to shift under the weight of Miriam's unyielding resolve.

"This cycle ends now," Miriam whispered.

And with that, the stone beneath them glowed, its symbols blazing to life in a brilliant, blinding light. The ground trembled as if the land itself was alive, a powerful force awakening. Dana stood still, feeling the connection to everything around her—every thread of reality seemed to snap into place, a realization flooding her mind as the energy surged.

The light expanded outward, washing over everything in its path. Hollow's figure flickered violently as the energy tore at the fabric of his being, the once-unyielding presence now feeling unstable. His eyes narrowed as he struggled to maintain his form, his movements growing more erratic.

Dana's breath caught as she realized what was happening. This wasn't just about breaking the cycle anymore. It was about unraveling it—shattering it entirely.

And Hollow was no longer in control.

The light continued to pulse, a heartbeat of energy that rippled through the ground, through the trees, and even through Dana herself. She felt it—she felt every shift, every unraveling piece of reality as if the world was being rewritten before her eyes. The stone at the center of the clearing glowed brighter, casting a powerful light that seemed to drown out everything else, until even Hollow's shadowed form began to fade into the brightness.

Hollow's figure trembled as the light pressed in, his form buckling under the weight of the reality-shifting force. His eyes, once burning with cold calculation, flickered with something almost human—fear, perhaps, or an acknowledgment that his grip on the cycle was slipping. He took a step back, but the ground beneath him cracked, and the very air seemed to reject his presence, pushing him further away from the center of the stone's glow.

Hollow's form flickered again, this time more violently. His dark figure was dissolving, the edges of his body breaking apart under the weight of Miriam's power. The air around them crackled with intensity, a final confrontation between two forces that had shaped the fate of Pine Hollow. Hollow's hands, once steady and commanding, trembled as they reached for the edges of the light, trying to push it back, but the more he resisted, the stronger Miriam's force became.

The stone beneath Miriam's feet seemed to pulse in rhythm with the energy surrounding them, its ancient symbols glowing brighter with each passing second. The ground around them vibrated like the earth itself was surrendering to the unrelenting energy that Miriam controlled.

It was as if the entire town, the entire cycle, was being stripped away, piece by piece, and Hollow—once the master of this reality—was powerless to stop it.

The clearing around them felt as though it was being peeled away, layer by layer. The very air shimmered, pulsing with the raw energy radiating from Miriam's presence. The towering trees that once loomed like silent sentinels were now shifting, flickering between moments in time, their outlines stretching and collapsing as though caught in the wake of something far greater than themselves. The night sky above warped, stars bending in unnatural arcs, as if the heavens themselves were witnessing something they were never meant to see.

Hollow's shadowed form twisted violently, the darkness that made up his body writhing as the cycle buckled under the force of Miriam's unraveling. His face contorted, mouth open in a silent scream as the light pressed against him, driving him back toward the edges of the clearing. His movements were no longer deliberate—no longer controlled. He staggered, his once-imposing presence now flickering, unstable, like he was being reduced to something less than the force he once was.

Miriam did not falter.

She stepped forward, and the ground trembled beneath her feet. Every movement she made, every breath she took, carried with it a command—an inevitability. Hollow had once been the architect of the forgetting, a force beyond comprehension, but now, as the weight of the unraveling cycle bore down on him, he was nothing more than an echo of his former power.

Dana watched, unable to move, unable to speak. She could feel the shift in the air, the way the cycle itself seemed to be pulling apart at the seams. The Watchers had rewritten reality over and over again, but now, under Miriam's unwavering force, the ink was running, the pages unraveling. And Hollow, the one who had held the pen, was being stripped of his control.

Hollow's flickering form lunged forward, desperation clawing at the space between them. He reached toward Miriam, fingers stretching impossibly long, his presence warping the air around him. But the moment his hand reached the threshold of her light, his form spasmed, recoiling as if burned. A deep, guttural sound—more than a voice, less than a scream—escaped him, his entire being trembling under the weight of the inevitable.

"You do not belong here anymore," Miriam said, her voice like the wind over the sea, steady, unshakable.

With a final, deliberate motion, Miriam raised her hand, and the clearing erupted with blinding radiance. The ground cracked beneath Hollow's feet, the air filled with a deep, resounding hum, as though the very fabric of existence was exhaling in relief.

Dana could do nothing but stare as Hollow's form flickered one final time. The shadow that had loomed over Pine Hollow, over the cycle, over her life—began to collapse inward, consumed by the weight of the unraveling. He let out a sound—half snarl, half something else—before his figure collapsed into itself.

And then, just like that, he was gone.

Silence followed.

A stillness that felt foreign in the aftermath of something so immense.

The air around them was different. Lighter. The tension that had clung to Pine Hollow like a second skin was peeling away. The trees no longer flickered between moments in time, and the stars above no longer bent unnaturally. Reality was settling, shifting, stabilizing in the wake of Hollow's absence.

Miriam lowered her hand, her glowing eyes dimming just slightly. She turned, and for the first time since revealing her true form, she looked at Dana.

"It's not over," she said.

Dana's breath caught.

Because she knew, deep down, that Miriam was right.

Hollow was gone.

The cycle was breaking.

But she still sensed… something. Something growing.

The air around them remained charged, humming with residual energy from what had just transpired. The forest no longer pulsed with the suffocating weight of Hollow's influence, but there was still something unsettled in the atmosphere—a waiting, lingering presence that had yet to fully dissipate. The cycle had been severed. Dana could feel it, the same way she had felt every shift, every unraveling thread. But there was also something underneath the unraveling of Hollow and the Watchers. Something ancient. Something not dissipating, but developing.

Miriam stood still, her form still flickering slightly as if the immense power she had wielded had not yet settled back into its dormant state. Her gaze lingered on Dana, unreadable, as if weighing something she had not yet spoken aloud. Then, slowly, her glowing eyes shifted toward the stone. A large crack seemed to be forming at the top. The runes carved into its surface were no longer alight; their energy had been spent in the confrontation. But Dana understood—this was not the end. It was the beginning.

The weight of that realization settled deep in Dana's chest. They had done something—something irreversible. The air still pulsed with the remnants of Miriam's power, but it wasn't victory she felt. It was change. A shift in the foundation of everything Pine Hollow had been built on. The cycle was breaking, unraveling—but if Miriam had severed one thread, Dana wasn't sure what remained beneath it.

Caleb groaned beside her, stirring slightly. His body twitched, his fingers digging into the dirt as he struggled to push himself up. Dana immediately dropped to his side, her heart still pounding. "Caleb?" she whispered, her voice raw. He blinked rapidly, as if clearing static from his mind, but his face was pale, his breath shallow. "What… what happened?" His voice was hoarse, as if something had been taken from him and only now returned.

Dana swallowed hard, steadying herself. "It worked," she murmured, barely believing the words herself. "Miriam—she—" Dana turned her gaze back to where Miriam had stood, where Hollow had fought against the unraveling force of the cycle. The clearing still hummed with residual energy, but the figures were gone. The stone at the center remained, its symbols dimming now, as if it had expended its power. The crack growing and traveling further down.

Caleb groaned again, pushing himself upright with effort. His eyes flickered around the clearing, confusion furrowing his brow. "Where is she?" he rasped. "Where's Hollow?" Dana didn't have an answer. There was no trace of them—no lingering presence, no final warning from Hollow, no lasting imprint of Miriam's overwhelming power. It was as if they had both been swallowed by the cycle itself, erased in a way even the Watchers couldn't undo. But something about that didn't sit right. Miriam wouldn't just disappear. Not like this.

Dana swallowed hard, scanning the clearing for any sign—any lingering presence, any ripple in the air where Miriam or Hollow had stood moments before. But there was nothing. The stone beneath her feet was still, the energy that had once pulsed through it now dormant, as if the confrontation had drained it of whatever power it once held.

Caleb pushed himself up, still unsteady, rubbing his forehead like his skull was full of static. "This doesn't make sense," he muttered. "She wouldn't just—" He stopped, exhaling sharply, like the weight of everything had just hit him at once. "Did she—did she win?"

Dana wished she could give him an answer. But her gut told her it wasn't that simple. The cycle had been built on something deeper than just Hollow's control—it was woven into the town, the land itself. Even if Miriam had defeated Hollow, and the cycle was broken, that didn't necessarily mean the town was safe.

"I don't know," Dana admitted, her voice hollow. "But I think—"

She turned back toward the stone, hesitating before reaching out. When her fingers brushed the surface, a strange pulse vibrated through her bones—not the same overwhelming force she had felt before, but something quieter, like an echo of what had been.

Caleb took a shaky breath. "And the cycle?"

Dana let her hand drop to her side, her jaw tightening. "It's broken."

Caleb frowned. "So that's it? Miriam saved us?"

Dana closed her eyes for a moment, trying to tune into the feeling in the air, the weight of everything shifting around them. "I don't think so. Hollow was a part of it. A major part of it. The protector of the cycle, the now cracked stone, the Mother of Pines ..." her voice trails off.

"What is it?" Caleb asks.

Dana turned to face him, her voice steady despite the exhaustion settling into her bones. "No, it's not over yet."

The forest around them felt... unsteady. The edges of the clearing seemed to shift, the trees warping subtly, as if adjusting to a new shape. The Watchers' grip had loosened, but something else was shifting in its place, something Dana couldn't quite define yet.

Caleb glanced over his shoulder, scanning the trees like he expected something to lurch out of the darkness. "Then what the hell do we do now?"

Dana hesitated. For the first time, she didn't have an immediate answer. The pull that had guided her here had faded, leaving only instinct. But she knew one thing for certain—Miriam was gone, and that meant whatever came next, they were on their own.

She looked back at the stone one last time. The stone now had a large singular crack from top to bottom as if it was hit by a massive axe. The symbols carved into its surface had dulled, no longer glowing, no longer humming with energy. But they weren't erased. They were still here, still part of whatever remained.

"We figure out what's left," Dana said finally, adjusting the strap of her bag. "And we finish what she started."

Caleb sighed, dragging a hand down his face. "Great. Just great."

But he didn't argue. He fell into step beside her as they turned away from the clearing, heading back into the shifting, uncertain woods.

And as they walked, Dana couldn't shake the feeling that something—**or someone**—was still watching.

Caleb walked in silence beside Dana, his eyes darting between the trees like he expected something—anything—to jump out at them. The quiet was wrong. The air was different now, lighter, but not entirely free of the weight that had settled over Pine Hollow for so long.

Dana felt it too. The shift. The absence of Hollow, of Miriam, had left a void in the world, one she wasn't sure how to fill. The Watchers weren't gone, but they weren't pressing down on them like before. The reality of what had just happened still hadn't fully sunk in.

She pressed forward, leading them away from the clearing, though every step felt aimless. They were alive. But what came next?

Caleb finally broke the silence. "You think she's really gone?" His voice was quiet, almost like he was afraid saying it too loud would make it real.

Dana swallowed, keeping her gaze forward. "I don't know."

Caleb exhaled sharply, shaking his head. "This is bullshit. She drags us into all this cryptic nonsense, helps us just enough to survive, and then what? She just disappears?"

Dana felt his frustration. It was her frustration too. But she had spent enough time trying to understand Miriam to know there were no easy answers.

"I don't think she had a choice," Dana muttered. "Also, I don't think she left us with nothing."

Caleb scoffed. "Yeah? Feels like nothing."

Dana stopped walking.

Caleb took another step before noticing, then turned to face her. His face was drawn, exhausted, but there was still fire in his eyes.

"She changed things," Dana said. "Whether or not she planned to, she changed things."

Caleb rubbed his hands over his face. "You keep saying that. But how do you know?"

Dana hesitated, then turned her gaze toward the trees, focusing on the quiet hum in the air. It wasn't the same as before. The weight, the grip of something unseen—it was weaker now. Hollow's hold was broken.

She looked back at Caleb. "Because I can feel it."

Caleb's jaw tensed, but he didn't argue. He just sighed and started walking again, mumbling, "I hope you're right."

Dana followed, adjusting the bag on her shoulder, feeling the weight of the files inside. The answers they had stolen, the proof of everything her mother had known. They had work to do.

They just had to survive long enough to do it.

They reached the edge of the woods before the sun had fully risen, its first light filtering through the trees like gold-dipped shadows. Pine Hollow stretched ahead of them, eerily quiet.

Dana slowed, scanning the road ahead, the buildings beyond. Something about the town felt... off. It wasn't obvious, not at first, but the longer she looked, the more the details began to shift in her mind.

The diner on the corner, the one that had been boarded up for as long as she could remember, now had lights flickering inside. The old hardware store, its sign faded and half-collapsed, was suddenly pristine—untouched by time.

Caleb noticed it too. "Uh... Dana?"

She kept walking, her pulse quickening as she scanned every street, every building. It was all just *slightly* wrong. Not different enough that someone who lived here wouldn't recognize it—but different enough that **she** knew.

Reality had shifted.

Caleb stopped in the middle of the street, turning in a slow circle. "This is—this is not right."

Dana clenched her jaw. "No. It's not."

It wasn't just that the town had changed. It was **rewriting itself**. Like something was trying to put the pieces back together. But not in the way they had left them.

Dana ran a hand through her hair, exhaling sharply. "We need to find somewhere safe. We need to—" She stopped, her gaze locking onto something down the street.

A car.

An old police cruiser, parked just ahead. A cruiser that shouldn't exist anymore.

Dana's pulse pounded in her ears. Because she knew that car.

She **knew** it.

And the sight of it sent ice crawling down her spine.

Ben's car.

Caleb turned to Dana, his voice low, cautious. "What is it?"

Dana didn't answer. She just started walking. Dana's steps were slow, cautious, as if she thought the car might vanish the moment she got too close. Her pulse pounded in her ears, drowning out everything else—the night air, Caleb's breathing behind her, the soft hum of Pine Hollow's unnatural quiet.

But the car didn't disappear.

It stayed.

Waiting.

Her fingers hovered just over the door handle, hesitant, unsure. Every part of her screamed that this wasn't possible—that she *knew* what had happened, that Ben had been erased, wiped from existence.

But here it was.

His car.

Not abandoned, not rusted over with time, not a relic of a past that had been scrubbed clean. It looked like it had never left. Like it had been here *the whole time.*

She swallowed hard, finally pressing her palm flat against the cool metal of the door. It was solid. *Real.*

A cold dread crept into her gut.

Behind her, Caleb shifted uneasily. "Dana," he said, voice low, cautious. "Are you gonna tell me what the hell is going on?"

She barely heard him. Her focus was locked on the car, on the small details that shouldn't be there. The coffee stain on the dashboard, the scratch by the driver's side mirror—things so minor, so *insignificant*, but impossibly, terribly *right.*

Her throat tightened.

This wasn't a mistake. This wasn't something the Watchers had forgotten to erase. It was something they had *put back*. And that terrified her more than anything.

Her fingers curled around the handle. She pulled. The door opened with a quiet *click*, the sound sharp in the silence.

The interior smelled the same—faintly of old leather and something distinctly *Ben*.

She took a quick breath.

The keys were in the ignition.

Waiting.

Caleb took a slow step closer, his tone measured. "Dana, you're freaking me out a little here. What is this?"

She swallowed, her voice barely above a whisper.

"It's Ben's car."

Caleb blinked. "Who the hell is Ben?"

Dana felt like the world dropped out from under her.

She turned to look at him, the words knocking the breath from her lungs.

He didn't know.

He didn't *remember*.

The realization hit harder than she was prepared for.

Caleb had gotten his memories back. He'd remembered *everything* the Watchers tried to take from him.

But not Ben.

Ben was still gone.

Still erased.

Even from Caleb.

Her stomach twisted violently.

This wasn't the same as the missing people. The ones who had been taken and *kept*, the ones Caleb had started to remember.

Ben wasn't *kept*.

Ben had been wiped away completely... by Hollow.

Since Hollow is gone, is that why his car is back?

Her fingers gripped the edge of the open door, trying to ground herself. "He was—" Her voice faltered. "He was the sheriff."

Caleb frowned, skeptical. "No, he wasn't."

Dana inhaled sharply. "Yes, he was."

Caleb's confusion deepened. "Dana, Sheriff's been the same guy for *decades*. I met him."

Dana shook her head violently, panic clawing at her ribs. "No. That's *not* right."

But it *was* right.

For Caleb.

For everyone else.

Because that was the version of reality the Watchers had rewritten.

Her hands trembled.

But the car—

The car was proof that something had changed.

Something was *cracking*.

Something was trying to push through.

She turned back to the open door, heart hammering. The keys were right there.

Waiting.

She reached out—

The second her fingers brushed the key, a *shock* jolted up her arm.

Dana gasped, stumbling back as a sharp pain shot through her skull, vision swimming.

For the briefest second—

She *heard* something.

A voice.

Familiar.

Distant.

Dana.

She sucked in a sharp breath, eyes wide.

Her pulse was a drumbeat in her ears, her skin buzzing with something she *didn't understand*.

Caleb caught her arm before she could fall completely. "Jesus—Dana, what the hell was that?"

Dana barely registered him.

She turned back to the car, heart in her throat.

Nothing had changed.

But she knew what she heard.

She *knew*.

Her grip tightened around Caleb's arm.

"We have to find him."

Caleb stared at her like she'd lost her mind. "Find *who*?"

Dana's jaw clenched.

She turned to face him, eyes burning.

"Ben."

Epilogue

The sky over Pine Hollow had shifted. The air, once thick with the weight of something unseen, now felt thinner, lighter—but not in a way that brought relief. The oppressive presence that had clung to the town for centuries had lifted, yet Dana couldn't shake the feeling that something else had taken its place.

She stood at the edge of the woods, her fingers curled tightly around the strap of her bag. The morning light cut through the trees in unnatural slants, painting long, distorted shadows across the dirt road. She should have felt victorious. The cycle was broken. The Watchers, Consequence, Hollow... or the Mother of Pines... was gone.

And yet, she had never felt more unsettled.

Behind her, Caleb leaned against Ben's car—the car that shouldn't exist. He had spent the last hour rifling through it, checking the glove compartment, the trunk, the seats, searching for any proof of the man he had once known. But every document, every scrap of paper, was blank. The car was real, but Ben wasn't in it. Not yet.

Dana turned her gaze back to the road ahead. She hadn't slept. Her mind wouldn't let her. Every time she closed her eyes, she saw the flickering remnants of Hollow, saw the light swallowing the darkness whole. But there was something else, too—something she hadn't told Caleb. In that final moment, when the Watchers' grip on Pine Hollow had shattered, she had felt it. A ripple, a tearing sensation, like the weight of something shifting, something pressing against the edges of reality. Something she didn't understand.

She didn't know what it was. Only that it had been held at bay by the very thing she had destroyed. And now, there was no one left to tell her what she had set free.

A chill ran down her spine as she remembered Miriam's warning. **"You assume it can be stopped without consequence."** At the time, Dana had pushed forward, too desperate for answers to stop and consider the weight of Miriam's words. But now, standing in the aftermath, she understood. The cycle had never just been about Pine Hollow. It had a deeper purpose. One only Miriam knew.

And if she was still alive, Dana would have to find her. But she kept that to herself.

A wave of nausea rolled through her suddenly, sharp and unexpected. She inhaled through her nose, pressing a hand against her stomach as she steadied herself. It wasn't just exhaustion or stress. A different kind of knowing settled in her bones, slow and undeniable.

She was pregnant.

The realization sent a shiver through her. It didn't make sense—none of this did. But somewhere, deep in the part of her that had always known the Watchers were real before she had words to name them, she understood. This was why she had survived when she shouldn't have. Why she had resisted the forgetting when others hadn't. Why she was still standing when Hollow had tried to erase her.

Ben's child had tethered her to something stronger than the Watchers' reach.

Dana swallowed hard, forcing her expression to remain neutral. She couldn't tell Caleb. Not yet.

"We need to find him," she murmured.

Caleb looked up from the car. "Ben?"

Dana nodded, her grip tightening on her bag. "If he's out there, we have to bring him back."

Caleb exhaled, rubbing his temples. He glanced at the car, then back at Dana. "You really think he's still him?"

Dana didn't answer right away.

Caleb swallowed. "Because I don't think I was."

Dana shook her head. "I don't know. But we have to try."

A gust of wind moved through the trees, colder than it should have been. The birds had stopped singing. The silence stretched, deep and unnatural. Dana's breathing stopped as she glanced toward the tree line, her pulse kicking up.

Something was watching. Not the Watchers. Something worse.

Caleb followed her gaze. "Dana…?"

She shook her head, forcing herself to breathe. Not now. Not yet.

"Let's go," she said. "We don't have time to waste."

She turned toward the car, pushing down the gnawing sense of unease twisting in her gut. The cycle was broken. The Watchers were gone.

But something else had woken up.

And Pine Hollow was far from safe.

Made in the USA
Columbia, SC
12 March 2025